THE COMFORT OF A KISS

"Close your eyes for a moment," he murmured.

"No . . . no, I should be getting back up to Delphine." She tried to rouse herself, but he kept her there by the fire, and she stopped resisting.

"She's sleeping, likely," Charles said. "The servants know where you are, and your maid will take care of her."

"Lundy is more than sensible. She saved my life when I was ill after having Delphine."

"Then the child is in good hands. And so is her mother. Rest, Nell."

His hands moved again to her back and massaged. She closed her eyes and drifted hazily.

"Come, lean against me and close your eyes for just a minute."

Relaxing back against his shoulder, she closed her eyes again. When she felt soft lips against hers, she opened her eyes and stiffened, gazing into his eyes with alarm, but he murmured against her mouth, and kissed her so tenderly that she surrendered to how unexpectedly sweet the caress was . . .

Books by Donna Simpson

Lord St. Claire's Angel

Lady Delafont's Dilemma

Lady May's Folly

Miss Truelove Beckons

Belle of the Ball

A Rake's Redemption

A Country Courtship

A Matchmaker's Christmas

Pamela's Second Season

Rachel's Change of Heart

Lord Pierson Reforms

The Duke and Mrs. Douglas

The Gilded Knight

Published by Zebra Books

THE GILDED KNIGHT

DONNA SIMPSON

ZEBRA BOOKS
Kensington Publishing Corp.
www.kensingtonbooks.com

PROLOGUE

Lady Nellwyn Simmons drew the covers up to her daughter's chin and settled down on the bed next to her. To tell this story she had no need of a book. It was a tale so old and so well worn that she could recite it by heart. "Once upon a time . . ."

"Mama," Delphine said, staring up at her mother, her blue eyes bright and alert, "why do all fairy tales begin with Once Upon A Time . . . ?"

Nell, as she had always been known to those who loved her, repressed a smile. Her daughter was engaging in the time-honored custom of extending bedtime. "Just because it's so, Delphine. It just means that it happened once, a long time ago."

"Oh. All right."

Nell went on.

"Once upon a time there was a handsome, brave, and gallant knight, and his armor was all of purest gold, so pure and bright it shone in the winter light and rivaled the sun itself for brilliance. He was known as the Gilded Knight because of that gold armor, and he was very proud of it, shining it every day, a task he would not even let his squire take care of."

"Mama, would gold armor be strong?"

"I don't know, Delphine. Now hush so I can tell the story."

"Now, in the kingdom next to the knight's there was a beautiful princess in a tower. How she got there, no one knew, and no one could say how to get her down.

"A dragon kept her there, a selfish, evil old dragon with a scaly back and pointy, dripping fangs, red eyes, and fire for breath. He wanted the lovely princess for himself and kept her in the tower just to look at and admire her golden hair as it sparkled in the sun."

"Was her hair like yours, Mama?" Delphine murmured, fighting sleep but sounding drowsy.

Nell smiled into the dimness and stroked her daughter's cheek. "No, much prettier and softer . . . more like yours, precious."

"Oh. Why did the dragon want her for himself? He didn't love her . . . did he?"

Such a good question. Nell bit her lip. "I don't know why the dragon wanted her, darling. Sometimes people . . . and dragons, I suppose . . . just want something they think others will want. They only want it because it is supposed to be valuable."

"I don't understand." Delphine had awoken again, as she always did when a subject interested her. And an unanswered "why" always interested her.

"Neither do I understand. But we can't understand everything in the world." Lord knew that was a lesson she had had to learn in the long years of trying to figure out her late husband and his behavior. Finally she had given up and relegated all her unanswerable questions and doubts to some place in her mind where she stored that which was not worth the effort to figure out.

"Why not?"

Ah yes, the question related to the "why" question. "Why not? It's just so." She gazed down at Delphine and stroked her hair. Even by the dim candlelight, the white-gold of her daughter's hair gleamed. Her one and only surviving child, she was more precious to Nell than anything or anyone in the world. "Some things we can figure out if we try. Some things we don't understand until the right moment. And some things we may never figure out."

"How do we know the difference?"

Nell sighed. That was a question for a philosopher. How did one know when something would forever defy understanding? And leave it to Delphine to ask such a question. And yet she was happy that Delphine was so intelligent and so inquisitive, and so she would never evade her inquiries. She stroked back her daughter's fair hair and tried to formulate an answer. And yet she was stymied. "Sometimes we don't know the difference," she said, softly. "All we can do is look in our own hearts, and if we think we have sought the answer, and yet it isn't given to us, perhaps it isn't for us to know yet . . . or perhaps ever."

Delphine nodded slowly, and her eyes drifted closed. "Oh."

Nell shifted her weight on the narrow bed and pushed her skirts down to cover her ankles against the wintry chill, which would not be completely dissipated despite the warm blaze in the small hearth. She glanced around the attic room, the slanted walls, the cheerful paper, the shabby but cozy furniture. The whole house was enormous, and if they had been fated to stay there for Delphine's whole life, as the daughter of the house she would eventually have been moved from the third-floor nursery down to the second-floor family bedrooms. But this was familiar, and given the events of the last year . . . there was no reason to change things now. But even this room, as well designed as slanted ceilings were to keep warmth in, was drafty. She would need to remind Martha, her daughter's nursemaid, to not let it ever get too cold. Some more coal on the banked fire overnight would help. Delphine must not get chilled.

Nell roused herself from dismal thoughts and went on with the story. "Where was I? Oh . . . yes, I remember." She hushed her voice and reassumed the proper tone for storytelling, which everyone knew was an awed whisper.

"The Gilded Knight adored the princess from afar and wanted to rescue her, but knew he was no match for a dragon with fangs and red eyes and fire for breath. And the dragon swore to burn down the knight's home unless he stayed away and never laid eyes on the princess again. But the knight's heart was sore, and he knew he couldn't leave her there alone and lonely. Even if he never had her for himself, even if he lost everything that was dear to him, he had to rescue her.

"So he fought the dragon. The battle raged for days and the knight's beautiful gold armor became scarred and battered and scorched. He came close to giving up; if he just left, he could still salvage some of his armor and perhaps repair it. But then he would remember the princess and would battle on for another weary day.

"And he won. Was there ever any doubt? If a heart is true and a quest just, if love is pure, then victory is inevitable. The dragon, humiliated and beaten, slunk away, and it is said that out of anger and pique it used its fiery

breath and exploded in a poof of smoke one day. The Gilded Knight built a ladder, scaled the wall, rescued his princess, and took her away to his kingdom, a fairy place of turrets and towers and lovely ladies and gentlemen who danced the night away in brilliant ballrooms. But not a one of the ladies was as fair as his princess, who proclaimed her love for him in front of all his family and friends, even in his battered and damaged armor. She didn't care. She said he was beautiful to look at because his golden heart shone through the blackened armor. The Gilded Knight was happy at last, having learned that love is worth any sacrifice, and that gold could not buy love. And so was the princess full of joy; she learned how much the knight truly adored her, that he would risk everything he loved for her happiness.

"*And they loved happily ever after.*"

"Mama," Delphine murmured, hugging her doll to her chest, "don't you mean 'lived happily ever after'?"

"No, they *loved* happily ever after," Nell said, standing and straightening Delphine's covers, tucking them up under her narrow, pointed chin. Candlelight flickered on the walls and shadowed the corners of the room. It was late, later than a nine-year-old's bedtime should be, probably. Roald, her late husband, had always accused her of being overindulgent with their daughter, and perhaps it was true, but she had her reasons. "Story time is over. You have to sleep, darling. Martha will be in soon and I'll have her bank your fire so it won't go out in the night."

Her daughter stared up at her, blinking drowsily, but determined to ask her question. "Does that ever happen, Mama? Do ladies and knights ever live happily ever after?"

Nell gazed down at the pinched, pale face of her daughter, and her heart constricted. The truth or a lie? She touched her hair and tweaked her cheek. "If you have someone to love, you will always be happy, like I am to have you," she said, preferring an evasion.

It was enough. Delphine closed her eyes and appeared to drift off to sleep. But when Nell reached the door, candle in hand, Delphine, her voice thick with drowsiness said, "I'm happy I have you to love happily ever after."

ONE

Lady Nellwyn Simmons, seated in the library reading letters, gazed out the diamond-paned window of ancient Meadow House and watched the nursemaid take her daughter, little Delphine, for a walk in the snow-coated garden. The walls of the old house were thick, made of ancient gray stone dredged from the earth hundreds of years ago, so the mansion was as much a part of the earth as the trees in the garden and the ivy that climbed its walls. Windows were deep-set, with a sill of a foot or more.

She stood, leaned over the desk, and scratched away at the thick coating of frost on the window, then pulled her gray merino shawl closer around her shoulders, shivering. It was frigid, as cold as January ever got; perhaps she ought to call them in. She chewed her lip in indecision for a moment, weighing the balance: health against enjoyment, overprotectiveness against a dangerous laxity. She worried that, given all the trouble they'd been through in Delphine's short life, she risked being so vigilant she didn't allow her child to be a child. She didn't want that for her daughter, didn't want her to be so sheltered she didn't enjoy real life. When Nell was a child she spent ten glorious years climbing trees, running free, playing tricks on the cook, outside more than she was in when weather permitted. Being sent off to school had signaled the end of such carefree days, and she still looked back with nostalgic delight on that period.

However, she had been healthy and robust, not like Delphine at all. Better to err on the side of safety. She put her hand on the latch, ready to open it and call them in, but just then Delphine ran and cried out in delight at the new appearance of her favorite statue in the formal garden. Nell drew her hand back from the latch. She would let them have just a few more minutes in the crisp air; she had not seen her nine-year-old daughter so happy for a very long time, not since before Roald died eight long months before, leaving her fatherless.

She watched Delphine and Martha, a smile lingering on her lips.

Delphine's favorite figure, mounted on a pedestal in the middle of the knot garden, was of a chevalier, a knight of old, his mighty steed pawing the air, his sword raised as if he was ready for battle. Delphine loved that old statue, though Nell never quite understood why. At one time it was perhaps a thing of beauty, but time and the elements had not been kind; it was grimy and green with tarnish, mossy and pitted with age. But now, with the January fog crystallized, an icy crust had formed and it glittered as the hard winter sunlight glanced off of it, making it appear carved from crystal. The day was waning and the sun setting early, as was its wont in early January, so close after the winter solstice. As old Sol descended, the rays turning golden, the statue took on that hue and looked gilded, like precious gold instead of dross.

A gilded knight, just like in Delphine's favorite fairy tale.

Nell leaned on the cold stone sill and held her breath, watching Delphine reach out, her upturned face rosy in the glow of the setting sun over the distant hills as she caressed with bare fingers the gallant steed and rider. Nell's breath caught in her throat and tears welled in her eyes; how she loved her baby, her precious child, and how close she had come to losing her far too many times, each time reminding her how frail and precious a gift was life. Delphine was occasionally sick with a mysterious fever, and each time had been worse; the only comfort their physician could offer was that the child might get stronger and grow out of the illness.

Or she might not.

Fear clutching her heart, Nell slipped the latch and pushed the window open. "Martha, Delphine," she cried, her words turning to frost even as she said them. "It's time to come in now. It's getting terribly cold!"

"Aww . . ."

"Delphine, now! Martha, bring her in, please."

"Yes, my lady," Martha said. "No more nonsense, now, Miss Delphine."

"And make her put her mittens back on! Lundy didn't make them for her just so she would not use them!"

"Yes, ma'am."

Nell pulled the window closed, her breath crystallizing in the cold air she had let into the room. As she pulled her shawl closer around her shoulders, she watched Martha bend over Delphine, pull the mittens on, and shepherd her charge toward the door. Delphine's cheeks were pink, glowing like burnished apples, and plumper than in the past. She had gained much needed weight in the last few months, though it had taken all of Nell's gift of persuasion to convince the nursemaid that something more than the traditional fare for a child, thin porridge and milk, was necessary, that meat and vegetables would not damage the poor dear's constitution and might even enhance it.

It had been a battle but with the conviction of right on her side Nell could do anything, especially where it concerned Delphine. And she had been right; Martha had capitulated completely even though her employer's logic defied every tenet of child-rearing she had ever been taught at her mother's knee. The nursemaid had explained to Nell that she had been taught that though children of the poor ate whatever was handy, children of the nobility were known to be more delicate. Her ma, Martha said, had told her that only white foods, like bread, milk, and porridge, were suitably bland for an aristocratic child. Anything heartier would putrefy in the little lady's stomach. The family's physician, Dr. Fitzgerald, was in complete agreement with Martha.

It was nothing Nell did not already know; after all, it was how she had been raised. But beef and vegetables were added to Delphine's diet, and she had thrived. Martha was won over.

As Martha and Delphine headed to the door, where a footman stood awaiting them, Nell sat back down at the low desk in her own tiny office—

she never used the library for her accounts or letter writing—and turned her attention to one particular letter, one she had been putting off opening. Her cousin by marriage, George, who also happened to be the new viscount barring any miraculous births from her—she grimaced at that ludicrous thought, given that Roald had been gone for eight months and that their relationship at the end had been more nurse and patient than husband and wife—wrote the most tedious, self-congratulatory letters. And even as he was praising himself, he always found a way to insult her. It was a feat of literary acrobatics that defied her ability to imagine a man so self-interested he could not see how he was affronting her.

Or perhaps his intent all along was to offend her, for he had openly expressed his hope that when she "deigned" to leave Meadow House, he would arrive to find everything named as part of the estate intact.

She remembered George and his younger brother, Charles, from their last visit to Meadow House, almost eight years before. It had been supposedly a congratulatory visit, to celebrate her daughter's birth, but to her at the time it had seemed more like an evaluation. Was she fit? Was she likely to bear Roald any more children? Would there be a male heir?

She had not been fit; she had been ill when they arrived, and had despised every minute of the occasions she had been forced to take part in. And she had despised both of them for being the reason she was at the dinner table instead of lying in bed in her chamber.

She broke the seal and opened it with a deep sigh.

After a brief perusal she tore it in half, strode across the room, and tossed the two pieces into the fire.

"Braxton," she said, raising her voice.

A footman entered and bowed.

"Braxton, please tell Mrs. Howard that we are to expect a guest soon. Lord Simmons has decided to send an emissary to make sure that Delphine and I not only clear out of Meadow House at the earliest possible moment, but that we leave with not a speck of furniture belonging to the estate."

She noted the tightening of the young man's expression, but well trained, he merely bowed and exited. Mrs. Howard, the housekeeper, would likely not be so circumspect.

So, George, sniveling coward that he was, would not come himself while she was in the house, but he would send his brother, Sir Charles Blake. What did she remember about Charles Blake from that last visit?

She cast her mind back that eight years to the last time she had seen him. It had not only been George and Charles who had been summoned to congratulate Roald, but all of his family. Among the guests, though, numbering ten or twelve, she did remember Charles Blake, probably because he was of all of the gathered family, as well as being the youngest, the very least prepossessing.

It was clear to her even if the servants had not whispered about it that Charles Blake was dissolute and useless, drunk all night and then suffering dreadful hangovers at the breakfast table. Sullen, but good-looking enough in a dissipated way, he coupled the Blake blond hair with unusual brown eyes. Lame in one foot, if she remembered right.

And hated his brother, it was obvious to her even in her own illness and depression. So what could have convinced him now to come on what was clearly a mission to rout her effectively from her home of so many years?

He must have changed, for back then his loathing for his brother had been crystal clear, as much as his antagonism toward the entire family. Or it could just be that now he was standing with his own family, presenting a solid front, as it were. That is what family did, so she had heard.

She stiffened her backbone. Though she had intended to leave Meadow House at the end of January anyway, now she had no intention of telling the emissary that. Let Charles Blake push, and they would see what happened then.

So far, Charles thought, crawling out of bed and facing the window of the bedroom in his rented suite in London, 1814 was turning out very much like 1813 had been: drab, monotonous, and as always, inadequate in every way.

And cold. He shivered and sat on the edge of the bed, his head in his hands. That his head was pounding should come as no surprise, given what he had consumed in the way of alcohol in the last twelve hours.

"Godfrey!" *Ouch!* His head hurt worse when he yelled like that.

His valet, neat of appearance even with a muffler wrapped around his neck, his lips compressed in a firm and disapproving line, appeared in the doorway. Charles glared at him, but then turned his gaze back down to the floor. Looking up hurt.

"Why is there no heat, Godfrey? I see no coal in my grate, but I certainly can see my breath." Charles pulled his dressing gown off the floor and wrapped it around him, burying his hands under his arms to try to warm them. "What's wrong, is the maid sleeping? And should you not have brought me my coffee half an hour ago?"

"There *is* no coal, sir, and the landlady says there will be no coffee, nor any other sustenance, until last quarter's rent has been paid. And she wishes me to tell you, sir, that she doesn't half like the duns coming to her door at all hours. You will settle your accounts, she says, or see the street face first." He paused for dramatic effect, and then went on. "Her son smiled when she said that."

Charles grimaced, shivered, and held his grumbling belly. The landlady's son was the proud and diligent owner of a farrier shop; his hands were as large as hams, and his temper was what was politely called "uncertain." That meant he brawled in the tavern every Saturday night. "I don't have any recourse, do I, Godfrey?"

"I beg your pardon, sir?"

Charles sighed. "I have to do George's dirty work. Have to go down to Gloucestershire and vanquish the enemy . . . slay St. George's bloody dragon in the person of a cold fish widow who won't budge from his inheritance. That was George's offer last night; that is my task if I am to receive a boon."

"If you don't mind my asking, sir," Godfrey said, advancing into the room and tidying the bedclothes, "why does he not just go down there himself? I have never known his lordship to shrink from claiming what is his own, by rights."

Charles roused himself from bed, chafing his arms and pulling his faded and worn dressing gown on properly, then belting it. "Ah, there's the rub, Godfrey. You see, the widow has a child—not a son, clearly, or old George would be out of luck—and the feeble little darling is sickly, feverish, ailing. Not all the time, but enough so that George is concerned for his own precious hide. As always, he is convinced that he is a frail willow, and that he will be struck down in the prime of his life by some dread disease or another. The Simmons Curse, he calls it, though old Roald lived to see his fiftieth year, and that is no youthful passing." Charles limped across the room, abhorring the cold that always made his lameness more pronounced. As his valet watched, he pulled the curtains open and gazed out on the frosty morn . . . or midday. London was icy and miserably lacking in warmth of any kind, female, familial, or meteorological. "If we want to see coal in the grate next week," he said, staring disconsolately out the window at the frost-coated world, "and the landlady smiling—in other words, to get George to pay off my outstanding debts—I will have to chivvy the widow and febrile infant out of Meadow House and to their London house. So George told me last night when I went to get his answer to my request for a loan."

"Why does he not resort to the law for relief?"

"Horrors!" Charles said, throwing his hands up in mock dismay. "The scandal! No, until there is no other way, George will not resort to the law. Family pride, you know."

"Shall I pack, then, sir?"

"Yes," Charles said, closing the faded curtain on the drab scene of London in early January. They were not in a good section of town, and the view was dreary and dirty, the street coated in a slushy frozen filth so dark it looked like mud. He sighed, his spirit sorely dampened. Bad enough he had been deputized to do the deed, but it would require effort to travel from London at the most miserable time of year, and not even to find any pleasure at the end, but just to return to a house he despised, to see a woman he remembered with distaste, and perform a service he found repellent and lacking in even the barest appearance of gallantry. He shrugged off his gloom. Did it matter really what he had to do? The end result, his debts paid and money in his purse . . . that was what he must think of. "There's nothing to stay here for anyway. Let us go and do the dirty work. With luck, we should be back in London in a se'nnight, and I can make old Lord Geoffrey's whist party with enough of George's precious gold in my pocket to strip the feathers off the downy old goose."

TWO

"You would have thought since I am doing my damned brother a favor he would have seen me conveyed in something better than this third-rate carriage he hired for my journey," Charles groused, as the carriage creaked and moaned over the rutted, frozen road in the dim light of twilight.

Godfrey, snoring in his corner of the dim vehicle, didn't answer.

Just as well, Charles reflected, staring out into the early evening gloom. He was in an uncharitable mood, having not even had enough money to drink the night before at the barely adequate country inn they had stayed at on the way north. He had had enough to order a frugal dinner and a pitcher of ale, which he had shared with Godfrey, and then had taken to his bed early. And because of his miserly brother, they had to make Meadow House by sundown, since he could not even afford another night at an inn. Perhaps George knew he would gladly have prolonged the trip if he had more money for another night at an inn and a few sovereigns with which to drink and gamble. Or more likely his older brother was just mean, in every sense of the word.

In good weather and with a well-sprung carriage they would have made it by midday, but the sky was lowering, threatening snow before long, and all was coated with a layer of ice that only got thicker as they traveled away from London. And the carriage was frigid inside, the warmth of the heated bricks the inn staff had provided him with that morning long having cooled. It made him anxious even to get to Meadow House, and that was enough to keep him musing on the vagaries of life, for he never would have expected to be impatient to get there, of all places, a scene of only humiliation and distress for him.

He glared out the window and recognized a turn ahead, the turn from the road to the long drive that wound up to Meadow House. His stomach clenched. Or perhaps he was wrong; he had thought they were there earlier, only to find himself mistaken. He wiped the frosted glass and squinted into the gathering gloom. But no . . . this time it was the approach, the long winding drive, he was almost sure of it.

He was just a child the first time he remembered seeing it, and his grandfather was awaiting his and George's arrival for a Christmas visit. His mother never made the journey due to her delicate health, or so she said, but with the wisdom of years Charles suspected she disliked her irascible father-in-law intensely, even as she saw the necessity of her sons staying in his good graces. Charles had been too stupid and naïve then, too young to know what awaited him at the hands of his cousins and their collusion with George. Ever after that he only dreaded the trip. School was bad enough; Grandfather's Christmas visits were worse.

Now he was an adult, though. He sucked his gut in and stiffened his backbone. He would have to steel himself for the coming week, for it wouldn't be pretty: a weepy widow and her feeble daughter, his demand that they leave forthwith, and a half-hearted offer to help them arrange their stay in London. It was not exactly a winter house party at a country manor; it was more like a morality play, with himself as the villain due to die at the end of the piece for his misdeeds. If he had any self-respect he would be ashamed to even be a party to such a knave's scheme, but he had long ago lost any pride he had been born with.

So he was the perfect fellow for the job. And that was a sobering thought, not one he wished to dwell on that moment. Instead, he must concentrate on assuming the correct frosty demeanor, suited to an eviction.

"Godfrey, wake up. We are arriving momentarily."

Nell, seated at the end of the dining table, watched Delphine anxiously. "Don't you like your dinner?"

Pushing the tender beef to one side, the child picked at a carrot. She shrugged and laid her fork down quietly. Her cheeks were pink and she was unusually silent, her blue eyes dull and her manner listless.

It couldn't be happening again. Nell prayed, *please, God, don't let it happen again.* But the pink cheeks, the silence, the sluggish movements—She leaned over to her daughter and pushed Delphine's hair back off her forehead, laying her fingers against the skin. Warm. Too warm. Maybe a good night's sleep—

"Adele," she said, to a waiting maid. "Can you call Martha? I think Miss Delphine is tired; an early night is called for."

"It's too warm in here, Mama," Delphine whimpered as the maid exited, her voice echoing off the high ceiling like a ghost's whispered conversation.

She wasn't going to wait, Nell thought, she would just take Delphine up herself. She scooped her reedy daughter up in her arms and carried her from the dining room through the great hall, headed toward the stairs to the sleeping chambers, when Braxton opened the front door and a gust of wind swept into the hall carrying a flurry of snowflakes with it.

"Close that door," she commanded her footman as two gentlemen strode in, stamping their feet and removing hats and scarves. She held Delphine against her, feeling her daughter's head loll on her shoulder. "Don't leave it open on such a night!" she scolded as she hefted her child in her arms.

The footman closed it and one of the gentlemen raised his head. "Ah, my lady, and how are you this fine evening?"

"Charles Blake?" she said, uncertainly. She had remembered a spindly youth, but this man was heavier. And yet he had the same tumble of dark blond curls on his forehead, though those were saturated with melting snow, and the same brown eyes.

"At your service, milady," he said, sweeping a low and ironic bow.

"You didn't dally a moment, did you?" she said, acerbically, shifting her daughter. Her icy words echoed off the dark paneled walls and up into the high gallery. "I only received George's letter yesterday morning. How prompt you are in the effort to eject me from my home."

If the widowed Lady Simmons expected him to look taken aback or abashed, she was to be disappointed, Charles thought, for he was delighted by the angry reception. It made this chore easier. He sauntered forward, determined to appear unaffected by her ire. He was hampered by the child in her arms, for he wished to take her hand and bow low over it, offering a chilly kiss on the back, as was appropriate to their cousinly relationship. "My dear brother must have anticipated my agreement to be his deputy, for he only informed me of my task Thursday evening, and here it is Saturday night, and I have arrived." Casually he said, "I suppose he wrote the letter to you before informing me of my charge."

"How prompt," she repeated, but with a less bitter tone. She stroked the head of the child in her arms and said, "I must get my daughter up to bed."

"Can she not walk?" he blurted, and then regretted his hasty words the next instant, seeing Lady Simmons's worried expression.

"Of course she can, she's just tired," the widowed viscountess said.

When she turned, Charles could see the child's face, the hectic pink of the cheeks, the glazed eyes. He frowned. "Is she not too heavy for you to carry, ma'am?" he said, his address more polite, more like his own natural tone. She looked too small and slender herself to be carrying the child. He stepped toward her. "May I help you?"

"No!" Her tone was adamant and her expression resentful, but with worry replacing the anger. Her eyes glittered in the poor light of the hallway as if tears stood in them, but her tone was cool and unaffected as she said, "Please, sir, make yourself comfortable in the . . . in the library. I'll be down directly."

She headed for the stairs and struggled up with her burden.

Charles watched her progress. She was still haughty, was the widowed Lady Simmons, but she was far more beautiful than he remembered, her pale hair like spun gold and her complexion creamy, not the sallow, hollow-cheeked look he remembered from eight years before. And her figure, judging from the contour suggested under the shifting gray of her dress, had matured too, to a ripeness far from the gaunt wraith she had been on his last visit so many years before. Still slender, she had blossomed into mature womanhood with enticing results.

"I suppose we must cool our heels," he murmured to Godfrey, who stood silently by. The footman still waited and Charles said, his voice raised, "As the lady said, we'll wait in the library. I would imagine Lady Simmons has assigned me a room; have someone see to our baggage, will you?" He surprised a look of thinly veiled animosity on the footman's face, and wondered at its cause. But the fellow just bowed and opened the door to the library for them, murmuring that he would send along some brandy.

Charles stepped into the chilly library. A maid hustled past him, lit some candles against the encroaching twilight, and stirred the banked blaze in the hearth. This was a properly run household, Charles thought, with a staff that knew how to treat a visitor. Not like George's London establishment, where visitors were reluctantly received and served warm tea and stale biscuits. How long would it take his brother to ruin this set of servants? Not long, Charles cynically reflected. His miserly attitude and irritable demeanor would soon drive them to hostility and defiance.

When the brandy was served and the room theirs again, Charles strolled the perimeter as Godfrey took a station near the fire and surreptitiously warmed his hands, clasping them behind him. "This was Grandfather's room," he said, pointing to the portrait above the desk of a stern, bewigged gentleman, comfortable paunch extending almost to his knees. "This was where he whipped me for playing the salted brandy trick." He caught his valet's mystified expression and held his glass up to the candlelight, watching the liquid glow a gorgeous deep amber. "Grandfather loved his brandy—he only bought from the best smugglers, and this is likely to be some from his vast store of it—and one day he found an entire bottle in his cellaret had been tainted with salt."

Charles remembered the roar of his grandfather's deep bass voice like an echo still in his mind. "Since George and I and my cousins were all staying here at the time, he knew one of us had played the prank, and I took the eventual punishment, which was my breeches hauled down in front of all the maidservants and my bottom caned until it bled." The sense of ill-use he felt as an eleven-year-

old came back so strong and bitter it was like a
whiff of sulfur.

"I assume, sir, that you didn't do it?"

"No, I didn't. George and my cousins did it, and
let me take the blame."

"And how old were you, sir?"

"I was eleven."

"Long time ago, sir."

Charles caught Godfrey's look. It *was* a long time
ago, and yet he could still feel the pain and humiliation as if it was yesterday. "It was a terrible
experience."

"No doubt, sir."

His valet's expression was impassive as always, but
Charles detected a hint of impatience. He felt the
urge to explain, and yet surely he didn't need to explain anything to his servant? It was beyond
ridiculous that he would even feel the need. Maybe
no one would ever understand what it felt like to always be the scapegoat, to always be the one who was
punished, sometimes justly, but usually unjustly.

He strolled to the window and glared out, not even
seeing the scene. He despised Meadow House, hated
everything about it, and yet he was there for a week,
at least.

The door to the library opened just then and the
widow entered.

"My lady. I hope I find you well." He could not
conquer his amazement at the transformation of
Lady Simmons; he remembered so clearly her
gaunt cheeks, gray skin, bony fingers. Now she was
radiant with thick lustrous blond hair and eyes the
piercing blue of a winter sky. Her pale skin glowed
with an almost pearly sheen. Why he had expected

her to still be sickly, he wasn't sure, maybe it was because of the reports of the poor health of her
daughter, but she was the very portrait of good
health and youthful vigor.

"I am always well, sir," she said, her manner stiff
and haughty. "May I belatedly congratulate you on
your knighthood, Sir Charles? I believe my husband was remiss when the honor was conferred. He
ought to have sent you congratulations and he did
not. I have always regretted that."

Charles watched her face for signs of derision.
"Thank you," he said, warily, waiting for some jest
or mockery.

"It was an unexpected honor, I understand?" She
strolled toward the fire, nodding at Godfrey who
faded away into the shadows. "One you earned
through some service to the Prince Regent?"

"Yes. Though he wasn't regent then, of course."
He turned, watching her progress. If she thought
he would offer the story of his knighthood up to
her, she was mistaken. It was something he rarely
spoke of, and certainly not to her. He gulped back
the rest of his brandy and set the empty glass down
on a table.

"Your family must have been very proud of you. I
believe your mother was still alive then?"

"Yes," Charles said through gritted teeth, wishing
she would leave the subject alone. "Oh, everyone
was terribly proud of me, especially my brother
George."

She gazed at him for a moment, her eyes fixed on
his. She turned to his valet then and said, "Godfrey,
is it?" The man nodded. "Braxton will show you Sir
Charles's rooms and you can make yourself and

your master comfortable. Just refer to Mrs. Howard, the housekeeper, for any of your needs."

Dismissed, Godfrey left the two of them alone. Lady Simmons indicated a chair by the fire. "Please sit, sir. I know we have much to discuss."

He glanced at the arrangement, changed since his last visit. Now two large chairs were drawn up in front of the fire, a thick rug before them, when in his grandfather's time all of the furnishings in the room were turned away from the hearth, as if the old man eschewed any hint that he needed its warmth. Now the large desk his grandfather had used was at the other end of the room in the shadows, relegated to second importance. It gave the once frosty chamber a different appearance, made it warmer.

Charles didn't take a chair immediately. Instead he watched the widowed viscountess while she drew the curtains, shutting out the view of wind flinging snowflakes against the window in the darkening twilight. Her movements were habitually elegant, but somehow nervous, a little quicker than necessary, somewhat jerky. If he had been gambling with her, he would have laid odds that she was not holding the cards she would have hoped for. And yet, what was there to be nervous of? She knew it was inevitable that she relinquish control of the Simmons estate. Old Roald had been dead for eight months . . . almost nine now. She was clearly not bearing an heir to the estate, and there were provisions for her and her child in the will. They had a house in London set aside for them, a comfortable house, with enough income for a staff. Charles knew all of this because of George's bitter complaints. He felt it should have all been his, even the part Roald was free to deed away from the estate.

And yet the widowed Lady Simmons was fretting. She finally took a seat. "What is your message?"

He followed suit. "My lady," he said, watching her eyes, the nervous flutter of one eyelid betraying her agitation. "I beg your pardon, but you know my message. George wishes to take possession of his estate, and though he is loath to impel you, he would like you to avail yourself of your own inheritance, Dorsey House in London."

"I would rather wait until spring. I would like to wait out my full mourning period here, in my home of so many years."

"With all due respect, my lady . . ."

She stood. "That is my answer, and you may take it back to George. If he is so set on having his house he can come and eject me himself."

She was trembling, and unconsciously perhaps, wringing her hands.

"My lady," he said, standing. Against all common sense he felt a kinship with her, and pity. "I feel that something is wrong. Please feel free to tell me if there is some justification behind your stubbornness, something George should know?"

"There is no reason but my own feeling that I deserve my full mourning, which will be especially hard to effect in London. You know, once one arrives friends call . . . and . . . and . . ." She sat down abruptly and put her face in her hands.

"My lady," he said, startled. He stood for a moment, undecided, and then knelt by her side. She was weeping, he thought, into her hands. Just as he had anticipated, a weepy female. "My lady, if there is anything . . ."

"Delphine is sick again," she said in a rush, staring past him at the fireplace. She shuddered. "She has been well for so long . . . I had hoped it was not true, but she is fevered, and it is so like the other times when she would go into a delirium. It's my own fault; I let her stay outside too long yesterday, and I knew better but she laughed for the first time since Roald . . . since her father died, and I just thought . . ." She broke down then, great gusty, heaving sobs that shook her body.

But she didn't cover her face again, and Charles watched, oddly compelled to not take his eyes from her, to absorb every moment of the twisted mouth and teary eyes, the nose quickly reddening with her sorrow.

Awkwardly, Charles patted her back. "She is likely just tired," he said. "I'm sure that by morning . . ."

"No, it's the same, I tell you," she cried, her voice thick and clogged with tears. "The same." She took a deep shuddering breath, and then more calmly added, "She's ill; I wish it were not so, but she is."

"What . . . exactly is wrong with her?"

"The doctor doesn't know. He says she may grow out of this . . . this periodic illness, but each time it seems to be worse to me, and I'm . . . I'm so afraid . . ." She broke down again.

Charles was just awkwardly patting her back, wondering if he ought to call her maid, when the lady stiffened and choked back her tears.

"I'm sorry, Sir Charles, for that outburst." She stood abruptly, brushed away the tears on her pale cheeks and patted down her gray skirts. "You will disregard it please. Perhaps we ought to speak tomorrow, if you don't mind. I'm sure you're tired, and no doubt hungry. You may dine at the table, or I will have Mrs. Howard send something up for you if you like."

She would not meet his eyes, Charles noticed. He had been thinking that the entire performance was calculated to give her leverage in her bid to stay at Meadow House until spring, but oddly, it was her abrupt recovery that made him doubt his cynical assessment. He was close enough that he could feel her tremble still.

"A tray for my manservant and myself in our suite would be sufficient," he said. He hesitated, but then said, "I hope your daughter is better in the morning, ma'am."

She looked up and there was such an expression of hope in her eyes it took his breath away. "It has happened so once or twice that she appeared to be getting ill, only to swiftly recover. I hope that will happen this time . . . oh, I do so hope . . ." She took in a deep, shaking breath, turned, and exited the library. "I will see you in the morning, then, Sir Charles. I trust you will sleep well."

THREE

Nell sat on a low stool by Delphine's bedside watching her sleep. Every yawn and sigh gave her hope with their normalcy, and then she would be dashed to despair by a fevered moan. Her child's cheeks were still flushed with color and her forehead damp.

How long this time? How long would she sit on this stool, praying, hoping, wishing for a miracle? In her baby's slight nine years there had been far too many hours spent there, far too many days with little sleep. Sometimes as she sat long into the night she felt like she was breathing for her child, willing her to continue with every intake of air into her own lungs. Exhaustion would overwhelm her, and she would imagine terrible things, that she was somehow responsible for her little girl's illness, that she was doing something horribly wrong and that every other mother in the world knew better, except for her.

She thought of her own and her siblings' upbringing; they had suffered the same benign neglect that others of her acquaintance had thrived on. She had seldom seen her parents, who had busy social lives, and had been relegated to the care of a succession of nannies and nursemaids, a tutor in her brother's case and a governess in her and her sister's, before she was sent off to school, where the care was little improvement except as far as discipline was involved.

And yet for all that she was rarely sick, with just the usual round of coughs, sniffles, and minor fevers. Why was Delphine so different?

But she was. From the day she was born almost two months early, her skin so pale and translucent Nell could see the blue veins threading across her skull, she had been fragile and prone to every illness possible. And from that very first day Nell had loved her so fiercely she knew she would die if her child died.

She reached out and touched Delphine's hair, as soft as fine silk thread. "We'll get through this, too, precious."

The door to the small bedchamber opened, letting a little of the light from the hall candle shine into the room. Light footsteps approached Nell from behind.

"My lady, you should go to bed and get some sleep. I'll stay awake with the little one."

Nell glanced up and smiled wearily at Lundy, her maid since she was a young lady just affianced to Roald. "I can't sleep yet. Come and sit with me for a moment."

Lundy took the chair by the window, and Nell remembered how that little woman—just a bare four-and-a-half feet tall—was the one by her bedside through her awful and painful labor and birth. Her husband was downstairs with friends hosting a card party that night—that was natural, since no one expected the father to be present at the birth—but when the birthing process was over his only question had been the sex of the child, and when he found she was a girl he did not even deign to visit his wife that night, but waited 'til morning. All that he said and did she had been told by the indignant house-keeper, Mrs. Howard, who even then was one of her strongest allies. Lundy, though, had remained silent, refusing to criticize the viscount, though she was tight-lipped whenever he came to see his wife and child over the next few days. When Simmons did visit her, all he said was "*Don't worry, we'll have a boy next time.*"

Next time! There had been no next time. She had been sick for a long time after the birth, and when she recovered it seemed something had changed within her body. No matter how much they tried—and Simmons began visiting her room again long before she wanted him to—she was never able to conceive again. Whether it was that fact that drove a wedge between her and her hus-band, or whether there was never much chance for a friendly marriage, she and Simmons never found any common ground and remained barely civil strangers for most of their wedded life.

And only civil because she was too caught up in her child's welfare to spare any time or thought for the state of her marriage. Maybe their estrange-ment toward the end was as much her fault as his, though she had never thought of it that way before. It was his behavior, after all, that had created the initial rift.

But through it all Lundy was there, steadfast, loyal, and sympathetic. She never criticized the vis-count, but she always supported Nell, knowing exactly what she needed, whether it was silence or chatter.

"Why don't you call Martha and have her sit with Miss Delphine?" Lundy said, finally, from the shadowed dimness. "And let me put you to bed. You'll wear yourself out with watching and worrying."

"Have you seen our company yet?" Nell said, preferring to ignore her maid's concern for the moment.

"I saw him in passing," Lundy said. "The new Lord Simmons's younger brother, I hear?"

"Yes."

"Come to throw you from the premises?"

Nell threw a swift glance Lundy's way. She well knew that woman's opinion that they should have left Meadow House in September. Perhaps she was right. They would have been in London over Christmas, and she could have reacquainted herself with some of her old friends. Gloucestershire could be lonely in winter, but it was a loneliness she was used to and rather liked. Perhaps that was unhealthy, but it was how she felt. "I wanted one last Christmas here," she said, in answer to her maid's unvoiced criticism. "It may be the only memory Delphine has of Christmas at Meadow House."

Lundy snorted. "Tell yourself what you must."

Nell stiffened and sat up straight. "You forget yourself."

The maid was silent, but stiff-lipped.

"I didn't mean that," Nell said.

"It's of no consequence." Lundy watched Delphine for a moment. "Do you think it's the fever again?"

"I don't know." Nell brooded for a minute,

watching the even breath puffing in and out of
Delphine's rosy lips. "She's sleeping quietly
enough now, but there is an occasional sign like
before."

"The fever?"

"Yes, and the restlessness. She was tossing and
turning a few minutes ago. But then she'll yawn
and turn over quite normally. I don't know what to
think."

"Are you going to sit up all night?"

"Will you have Braxton bring me a cot? I may
sleep here."

"I will. You know that young man would do anything for you."

"He is a good and loyal servant," Nell said, pur-
posely injecting warning into her tone.

"I said nothing," Lundy claimed, throwing her
hands in the air and clapping them down on her
knees. "But it would take a blind fool not to see that
young fellow's infatuation. Just a warning from an
old woman."

Nell sighed and shook her head. "Not now,
Lundy. I know Braxton is infatuated, but he never
by sign or word embarrasses me or himself. It will
pass. He's a young man, but not a foolish one." She
leaned over and felt Delphine's forehead again.
Was it her imagination or was she warmer than before? "I would that Sir Charles was not in the house
right now, not with Delphine maybe ill again. It will
be a nuisance, having company, and he with only
one objective, to get me out."

Lundy stood and crossed, putting one small hand
on Nell's shoulder. "I'll see what I can find out

about the fellow from his man . . . Godfrey, is it, the valet's name?"

Nell nodded.

"He's a good-looking fellow, though with mournful eyes. I shall have to see if Mrs. Howard thinks we should use extra precautions with the maids. Some of the young girls get silly, and we don't know his disposition."

Nell nodded again, not willing to worry about such things. Between them Lundy and Mrs. Howard would take care of everything, just as they always had. Nell had never replaced their butler, who died a few months before Roald; it hadn't seemed necessary in such a well-run house and with so few visitors.

When Lundy left, Nell watched Delphine for a few minutes and then set about making the room comfortable for her vigil. They were arrangements she had made many times before.

Charles sat and gazed out the window of his bedchamber at the moon sparkling off the snowy landscape. Aesthetically it was pleasing. When he was very young he had fancied himself a painter, and had studied for hours the natural arrangement of tree and hill and stream, finding in nature an asymmetrical beauty no landscaper's hand could ever duplicate.

He had even taken a few lessons from an art master—his mother's doing—and tried his hand at both the paper and the canvas. His ill-conceived amateurish renderings were likely long destroyed, the ones left at Meadow House, no doubt, by his grandfather who thought painting and drawing weak, feminine pursuits. Real art was immoral and foreign; just look at the chappies who did it, Grandfather would rail. Artists were all on the road to hell. The old man's ridicule and criticism had likely been one reason he had left off even trying. It was many years since he had lifted a pencil or brush.

Morosely he reflected that he had never been very good anyway, so it was no loss to the community of artists.

Godfrey entered and set down a tray. "The staff here is so very well-trained that even though they resent us profoundly, they still cannot resist performing their duties to perfection. This is the best beef I have ever seen, and the coffee smells wonderful. Your brother will ruin them."

"You're impertinent, Godfrey."

"I know. But truthful, sir."

"When George has all of this, I may decide to live here."

His valet dropped a cup and hastened to clean up the slopped coffee on the tray. "With your brother?"

Charles laughed and pushed his chair back onto its two back legs. "Wouldn't work, would it?" He let the chair thump back onto all four legs. "I dislike him and he despises me. And worse, this place has such awful memories . . ."

There was silence for a few minutes as Godfrey set up the tray on a table by the hearth. Finally he indicated to Charles his arrangement. "Dinner, sir."

"It smells good." He limped over and sniffed appreciatively.

"It is good," Godfrey said. "I got on the housekeeper's good side with a receipt for a cleaning liquid, and she gave me beef and ale and gossip. She is fiercely protective of her mistress, but apparently Viscount Simmons—the last one, not your brother—was not well liked by his staff."

"Really?" Charles sat down and dug into his dinner. "How do you know they like Lady Simmons so much?"

"Even when they don't say it outright, you can always tell. Mrs. Howard admires Lady Simmons. You will get no help in ousting her if the lady decides she wants to stay on until spring, as you indicated she said. They all love her."

"I was afraid of that." Charles ate for a minute in silence. The beef was fork tender, and roasted potatoes accompanied it. He had not eaten such a fine meal for years, it seemed to him. Even when he joined his brother for dinner, he was likely to get tough mutton and bitter coffee. When his hunger was sated, Charles hesitantly told his valet about Lady Simmons's emotional breakdown. "I thought at first it was meant to appeal to my sense of chivalry—she not knowing I have none—but . . . I don't think it was calculated at all." He considered that statement. "No, I don't think it was. Did you find out anything about the child?"

Godfrey, folding and putting away clothes in the clothespress, frowned, his pale forehead wrinkled in thought. "From what Mrs. Howard says Miss Delphine is often sick with a fever. Lately it had seemed the little girl was gaining in health due to her mother's persistent care, so it is thought, belowstairs, that this setback will be all the more devastating."

"So they already know she is sick?"

"Oh, yes. One of the maids, a girl named Adele,

was weeping about it. Very attached to the child, they are."

Charles finished his food and coffee and pushed away from the table with a sigh. "If I was not at George's mercy I would leave the woman alone. It may be unreasonable of her to want to stay here for another three or four months, but who is she hurting? Not George. How will it hurt him to stay in London 'til April? He is only put out because he isn't getting his own way. That has always peeved him."

"But your brother has made settling your debts contingent on expelling the lady."

Charles grimaced. "You don't have to make it sound so callous," he said. "Stop fussing with my clothes and go away."

Godfrey wordlessly finished his task, cleared Charles's dishes, and left.

Alone, Charles wandered over to the window again. He had to do this deed, and he needed to not feel any guilt. Well, that should be simple. It was time and past that the widowed Lady Simmons made way for the new viscount. Though Charles had made the point that George would not suffer by staying in London another three months or so, justice was on his side. The house was his. And it was not as if she was not provided for. She and her daughter would have a very comfortable home, Dorsey House, to go to. It was furnished and waiting, and she had a generous allowance to buy a new wardrobe for the end of her mourning period. He couldn't imagine why she was being recalcitrant.

He nodded sharply at his reflected image in the windowpane. She had it easy. His own allowance barely stretched to meet his needs, but hers, he happened to know from George's grousing, was bountiful . . . no, better than bountiful. Lavish.

She was just being stubborn.

He felt a twinge when he remembered her tears in the library, but pushed away the thought. On the morrow he would begin his campaign to oust Lady Simmons. If all went well, he and the lady and child could be back in London in a week, and he would be solvent again, with George's promised reward jingling in his pocket.

Then his life could continue on its habitual track, George would have Meadow House to himself, and Lady Simmons and her child—

They would be just fine.

FOUR

"Is Lady Simmons not joining me for breakfast?" Charles watched the maid bring in the silver pot of coffee for the sideboard, but asked the question of the very correct footman stationed there awaiting breakfast requests.

"No, sir," he said.

"What is your name?" Charles looked him over, thinking he was everything footmen were supposed to be: tall, straight, healthy, and handsome. Why it should be so Charles couldn't say, but it was. It was too bad the nobility could not be so chosen for certain qualities. If they could there would be no lame knights nor viscounts who fancied themselves ill at the first cough.

"Braxton, sir," the fellow said, in answer to his question.

"Well, Braxton, will you send someone to ask Lady Simmons if she will join me?"

"If you wish." The footman poured coffee into Charles's cup, and then filled his plate with requested items. "But she won't come down, sir," he finally finished, setting the plate in front of Charles on the rich, polished oak surface of the carved breakfast table.

"Why not?"

The footman stiffened. "I'm sure I don't know, sir."

"Yes, you do," Charles said, watching the young man as he plopped some sugar into his coffee. It was amazing to him that he even had coffee, for it was not a breakfast drink, though it was the one he preferred and had asked for. He had expected to have to make do with tea or chocolate, but it seemed, as Godfrey opined, the staff just could not help doing a good job even with a guest they disliked serving. Whatever he wanted was his for the asking. "You just said she wouldn't come down even if I asked her to, and that indicates to me you know her opinion on the matter."

"Not at all, sir."

Charles glared at the impassive young man's face. Impassive, and yet somehow resentment was delineated in even his stance. "Then I shall go and find her."

That shook the footman, and he stuttered into speech, saying, "S-she is with Miss Delphine, sir; the young miss is . . . is ill again."

Charles, in the act of standing, paused, then sat back down. "I had hoped that was not the case. I had hoped that after a night's sleep the little girl would be well."

"We had hoped so too, sir, all the staff. Miss Delphine is a favorite of everyone."

"Is she . . . often ill?" He asked even though he knew the answer, just to see what Braxton would say. He had never questioned a servant before, but had little recourse. In the whole of the house there was only him, Lady Simmons, and a throng of serving staff.

The footman pokered up. "Not my business to say, Sir Charles."

Shrugging, Charles turned to his breakfast and ate, wondering what on earth he would do during his stay. He was only to be there a week, at the outside, for that was the most time George expected him to take expelling Lady Simmons from Meadow House, but it was enough time to become thoroughly bored. It was the dead of winter, so there would be no sport, and he was not one much for hunting anyway, even if Roald Simmons's old game master was still up to it.

There was little society in the area, no complacent country squires to relieve of their gold in a game of whist, but the fortunate side of that was there were no simpering country squires' daughters to evade. Since his knighthood he had been subjected to his share of attention, and found it uncomfortable in the extreme. It was not that he did not appreciate the ladies, but he was drawn to a less coquettish and coy brand of female than the inevitable girls in their first or second season.

And he was not looking to get married anyway, though many of his friends had. He had never met a woman he thought he could stand to be tied to for life, and the thought of such a personal and interdependent relationship made him queasy.

He sighed, pushed his plate away, and glanced around. What now? A solitary game of billiards? A hand of solitaire? How long would he be mired in this dungeon without knowing if he would be successful or not?

If the staff were conspiring with Lady Simmons to delay him, he would end up looking like a fool. She could very well be using some mild indisposition on her daughter's part as a means to stall him indefinitely. Or maybe the child wasn't sick at all, just being used as a pawn in her mother's game.

Propelled out of his chair by that notion, he started away from the dining table and the staff began clearing the remains of breakfast before he even left the room. But Charles did not miss one worried glance by the young footman, who watched him leave the dining room and head to the stairs and the family wing. It could all be calculated as a stall. He would not be made to look or feel the fool this time; he would do what he came down to Gloucestershire for.

The upper hallway was dim and chill, no windows but one at the end of the hall lighting the carpeted passage. A startled maid stared at him from a doorway, clutching a stack of folded white linens to her chest. He cleared his throat. "I . . . uh . . . am looking for the little girl's room . . . Miss Delphine?" She gazed blankly at him, so he repeated, "Miss Delphine's room?"

"On the next floor, to be sure, sir," she said, her voice faint. "The . . . the nursery, sir."

The nursery? Wasn't she too old for the nursery? "Up?" He pointed to the stairs, where they narrowed as they climbed one more story, losing their carpet in favor of painted treads.

"Yes, sir."

As he began his halting ascent to the next floor he saw her, out of the corner of his eye, set down her stack of linens on a hall table and head for the back stairs. She was no doubt off to spread the news of his destination among the staff.

But he would not be deterred. As he clumped up the steps he was beset by depression, the feeling that he was on a fool's errand and he the equal fool for taking it on. No real man would act thus, he was sure. What else was there to do, though? He needed money to pay off his debts. There was never enough, but now that George was viscount and had access to all of the estate, he would surely help his brother live more comfortably than the meager stipend of a second son allowed?

And in return all he had to do was help his brother grasp control of that which he owned. There was nothing churlish about that, was there?

The upper hall was even more gloomy and uncarpeted, and led to another set of even more narrow steps that he thought, if he remembered right, led to the attic rooms of the older section of the manor. Outside the sun was beginning to break through the clouds, but little of that light reached here, in the cold upper reaches. He stared through the half light at the doors that lined the hall. Which would be the little girl's room?

Hearing a voice, a low soothing murmur, he moved down the hallway toward it. A door near the end was ajar; he poked his head in, surveying the interior. It was a cheerful room: papered slanting walls in a small, floral print, a white-painted hearth with a warm blaze in it and a lamp lit against the winter gloom. A small bed was on the outside wall. In the bed, well covered by covers and quilts, lay the child, and by the bed was Lady Simmons, sitting on a low stool. She was talking, telling a story, it seemed, from the rhythm of her speech.

The words were indistinct, but the tone was certainly gentle. His presence was intrusive; he would not be wanted here. But then Lady Simmons might never come out of the room all day long. Manners warred with need and self-interest won, as it always must for the impoverished.

He moved into the room, trying to make his gait more quiet on the polished wood floor. Lady Simmons turned and gazed at him, her expression impassive.

"How . . . how is your daughter? I was concerned, and the servants would not tell me anything." Not good; that sounded like whining. He cleared his throat. "I hope she is better." He steeled himself and woodenly moved across the room, moving a bundle of knitting and sitting down in a chair near the window.

Lady Simmons watched him silently.

He met her gaze, but then glanced past her at the child. She was a lovely girl, if he was any judge of children's looks, with wavy hair like spun gold, very much like her fair mother's locks, and his own, too. His child, if he ever had one, might look like Delphine Blake, for her face's shape was reminiscent of the Blake legacy.

Her thin form moved restlessly and Lady Simmons's gaze returned to her child. He watched the woman's face in profile, the dark circles under the eyes from a sleepless night, perhaps. In fact as he glanced around he could see signs that she had slept there: a cot pushed against the wall, the half-eaten remains of her breakfast on a low table by the cot.

"So," he persisted. "Is she better this morning?"

"She is neither better nor worse."

Her tone was cool and dismissive. He examined her face with curiosity, finding no trace of the sickly, teary, gaunt young woman she was eight years before at his last visit. Even with dark rings around her eyes she was a healthy vital woman now, life thrumming through her and pounding in the pulse at the base of her throat. Opening his mouth to say as much, he quickly snapped it shut again. That was no way to open the conversation; it would sound like he was wishing her ill, or blaming her for looking so healthy when her daughter was ailing.

Better just to come out with what he wanted. Sometimes forthrightness had a place.

"You said we would speak in the morning, my lady, but then you didn't come down to breakfast, so I thought I would save you the trouble." He tapped his fingers on his knee. "You must know that you cannot stay here until spring. It's not right, keeping the rightful heir from his inheritance. Your own sense of fairness . . ."

"Do not speak to me of fair," she said, her tone low and trembling.

"But . . ."

"No," she said holding up one hand in a halting gesture. She met his gaze. "You cannot mean to sit here by my ill child and ask me when I plan to leave Meadow House?"

"You have been stalling George for much longer than a few days, my lady. What would you have said to me if your daughter had not conveniently become ill?" He knew the moment he said it that it sounded heartless and cruel—*was* heartless and cruel—but there was no taking back the words. Her expression, so contemptuous, cut him to the core.

Her tone low and fierce, she said, "That is exactly what I would have expected George's brother to say and think."

"What do you mean?" He searched her eyes, the blue flintiness as cutting as a rasp.

"It is no less than the things your brother has accused me of in his numerous letters, starting the day after my husband's death was announced," she said, smoothing a wrinkle on the bed's cover. "I have put up with eight months of weekly letters imploring, exhorting, accusing, threatening, and insinuating all manner of things. Why I should have expected your approach to be any different, I do not know. The truth is, I will leave the moment I want to leave and not one second earlier. You may as well go now and take that message back to the new Lord Simmons, for it will not change."

He hadn't known about the many letters, if she was not exaggerating. What had George said in them? What had he insinuated?

Charles sighed and met her challenging gaze, staring for a long moment into her brilliant blue eyes, as wintry as the January sky. He was no interpreter of feminine expression, but there was something beneath her defiance, something he couldn't grasp.

The child moved and he glanced at the bed. Delphine Blake opened her eyes and stared directly at him just as the sun broke through the clouds outside and a beam of sunlight danced through the pane. She reached out one hand toward him.

He swiftly glanced at Lady Simmons and surprised

an expression of yearning hope as she gazed at her daughter; the longing in her intent stare twisted his stomach. When he met the little girl's eyes, it was to see a reflection of that yearning, a powerful expression of need. He moved forward to the bedside and knelt there, impelled by the force of the little girl's obvious want.

"Mama," she whispered. "The Gilded Knight, just like the story . . . he's golden." She touched Charles's hair, grasping a fistful.

"What does she mean?" he asked, terribly moved and frightened by that fact.

Lady Simmons, her voice thick, clutched her hands between her knees and said, "It is a character from her favorite fairy tale, Sir Charles . . . your hair . . . its golden color has reminded her of him, the Gilded Knight."

Silent, Charles stared down at the child, her blue eyes wide with wonder.

"Are you a knight?" the girl asked.

"Well . . ." He paused, taken aback, and then said, "Yes, actually I am."

She released his hair and clapped her hands together, her expression livelier than it had been just moments before and her gaze sharper, more focused. "Did the king knight you? With a big sword?"

"Uh," Charles stammered, "Something like that." He met Lady Simmons's gaze and shrugged, then looked back at the child. "Do you . . . do you want to hear about it?"

"Yes, please."

Charles awkwardly pulled his chair over to the bedside. When Delphine reached out her small hand and grasped his, he did not pull it away. The touch of her diminutive hand was comforting somehow, he wasn't sure why.

Nell, sitting on the low stool, her elbow on her knee and her chin in her hand, listened as Charles Blake related what was surely an idyllic and highly colored version of his knighthood ceremony. He was good at description and built a fairy palace with words, a court with lovely ladies and handsome gentlemen, courtly, polite, gowned in exquisite satins and lace. He related a touching and solemn scene, with himself humbled by the condescension of the royal family, who were grateful for his service to the prince.

But more than his words, she was fascinated by his face, the early signs of dissolution there, but still a softness and sensibility that she had not expected in the new Lord Simmons's brother. Holding Delphine's hand, he hunkered down beside the bed, and the little girl stared at him, the fever burning in her cheeks still, but serenity on her face.

Something had happened between Delphine and Sir Charles, something even Nell was excluded from. It made her feel a little lonely, but still fascinated.

As Delphine's eyes drifted closed, Sir Charles awkwardly released his hand from her grasp, and watched as she turned and hugged her blanket to her thin chest and slept. He stood and moved his chair back to the window, his limp pronounced, his expression thoughtful, his sandy brows knit. She had almost forgotten his lameness. Roald had derisively called his much younger cousin "Charles the Halt." Had others been as cruel, or perhaps worse?

"Thank you," she said, quietly, as he turned back to her.

"For what?"

"She's gone back to a peaceful sleep," Nell murmured, tucking the blanket in around Delphine's narrow form. "That's not always easy when she is fevered. You have a way with children."

"Oh, no, my lady, that can't be true. Can't say I have ever been so close to a child since I *was* one."

She repressed a smile. His denial was swift and sure, and yet his behavior with Delphine had been so natural and unaffected, not like an adult who was trying to be liked by a child, just one with a natural way he wasn't even aware of. "No, I suppose not. George has never married, nor have you."

"George will never marry unless he can be sure the lady is free from illness and has never suffered the grippe, ague, fever, or other contamination." It was said dryly, but with some bitterness.

"Is he so fearful?"

His expression became guarded. "He is . . . careful of his health."

Not having seen George for many years she had not been able to judge him, except by his fretful and fussy letters. This impression she had of the new viscount as a fidgety valetudinarian was confirmed by Sir Charles's words. "Is that why he sent you in his place?"

"Yes. He worries."

"But why did you come? Out of love for your brother?"

His reaction to her words was interesting, for he grimaced, then caught himself and smoothed out the expression of scorn.

When he didn't answer, she urged, "Is that it? A great love for your brother? Concern for his health?

A desire to please and indulge him?" She was deliberately taunting him, a method that often brought out the truth, no matter how cruel or shallow.

But he remained impassive now. "I only came to express George's wishes, ma'am, and to see why you have been stalling. Surely you must admit eight months is an excessive time for him to wait for his inheritance?"

"If he had not begun so quickly," she said, with a quick glance to be sure Delphine was still asleep, "when the first shock of Roald's death had not even worn off, I'm sure I would have been more amenable to an agreement as to the date of surrender of the estate and contents." The anger George had engendered always came back when she remembered his insulting letters, the tone of which became increasingly rancorous over the months. "You know your brother. Has he always been kind and considerate of you?"

She had hit her mark. Charles's expression darkened and he limped to stand and stare out the window. Why was he there, she wondered, if he was not happy with his mission? What did his brother hold over him?

At that moment Lundy slipped into the room, her curious gaze on Sir Charles. Nell bit back a smile, knowing her maid was likely the emissary of the staff, curious about the guest.

"Roads are bad," she said, quietly, to Nell. "And gardener says we are to have a foot of new snow by morning if he's not mistaken, and he rarely is."

Nell took the cue, stood, and crossed the room, standing in front of her "guest." "So, Sir Charles, unless you wish to be caught here for a time, you had best leave today with a message for your brother. You may tell him that I will leave when I want, and not a moment earlier."

He shrugged. "I have no pressing business my lady, and will be happy to accept your hospitality—or is it my brother's hospitality?—for a few more days."

FIVE

"Mama!" Delphine's cry broke the tension and Nell moved over to the bed, resuming her place on the low stool. Lundy, too, bustled over to the bedside.

Nell felt her daughter's forehead. "She's warmer," she said, looking up at her maid, her eyes tear-filled. "And there are some spots breaking out. Oh, when will that doctor get here?"

"The roads are terrible, as I said; I hope he is able to get through at all, my lady," Lundy said, retrieving a damp cloth from a bowl of water, wringing it out, and handing it to her mistress.

Charles hung back by the door and watched the two women attend the child, who was thrashing and moaning. Just a few minutes before she had been holding his hand and watching his eyes. He had felt some kind of connection, as little as he liked to admit it even to himself. But now she was incoherent; he felt helpless and extraneous.

"Would you please leave us, Sir Charles?" Lady Simmons said, throwing him an exasperated look.

"Certainly," Charles said, and exited. She was very high-handed, he thought, as he paced down the chilly hallway, ordering him around in a house that he was really more entitled to be in than she. If she

had left Meadow House when she ought to have
she would have access to much better medical care
for her child, and at a quicker notice.

And how contemptible of him to even think that
way, when he had earlier been speculating that she
was faking her child's illness just to justify staying in
Meadow House and not speaking to him.

He stopped at the large window at the end of the
hall and gazed out over the estate grounds. Snow was
coming down in sheets, drifting against the stable
buildings and box hedge. Pine trees in a grove at the
lower end of the garden were laden with clumps of
heavy snow, the dark green of their branches barely
visible through the thick coating of white. Even the
window was overlaid with a film of white, icy fingers
stretching beyond the crust of snow.

Winter had a chilly grip on the land and it
brought to mind his childhood friend, Roger.
Roger, a lieutenant in an artillery regiment posted
in the Canadas, had died early in the fighting there,
but he had written letters before his fatal engage-
ment with the Americans, and had complained of
the bitter cold and deep snow, so unlike the generally mild winters of home. He had harkened back
to their enjoyable times spent in London, living the
good life with other like-minded young men who
enjoyed the card table, good wine, and ladies of
complaisant temperaments. Even in winter one
could get about in London, and if company was
somewhat sparse, there still were always other
young men, avoiding their families, ready for a lark,
up for a night on the town.

But Roger was gone, buried in that cold winter
land, a casualty of a battle fought with too few

trained soldiers and too many farmers acting as militia. His family, beyond a brief period of mourning for him, seemed to have gone on without missing him overmuch. One less impoverished officer in the world, one less draw on the family coffer, seemed to be his father's attitude. Charles had been shocked and horrified, when he had gone to pay a visit to Roger's parents, that they were more interested in evaluating his own purse to see if he was a suitable match for Roger's younger sister, than in speaking of their lost son.

Charles bowed his head for a moment, thinking of his friend's engaging grin and carefree manner. He would always miss Roger. The world was a poorer place for not having him in it, but at least, despite what Roger's parents thought, his friend had made his mark on the world. He had served a cause that he truly believed in, defending Empire territory from the encroachment of the Americans.

It was 1814. Charles was almost thirty, and what had he ever accomplished in his life that was the equal of Roger's sacrifice, or . . . or Lady Simmons's gift to the world, her beautiful little girl? Barred from his desire to enter the army at a young age by his father's refusal to lay out the funds for a commission when, at eighteen, he had wanted to join with Roger—his esteemed father had thought the money would be a waste because of Charles's lameness—and never finding anything else worthwhile he could lend his hand to, he supposed he had just drifted into the role of dissolute gambler, as if he had no choice in the matter.

And now he was having to go, cap in hand, to ask George for help out of his debts, and made to push a defenseless lady out of her home of twelve years just to fund his habits. He didn't know what disgusted him most, his behavior, or his self-pity about his behavior. He behaved as though he had no say in the matter, that his path was preset. Was it? He supposed he had never questioned, just followed the easy way, the way of other young men of his status and rank. Most of his friends—those not inheriting the family title—were dependent in some way upon their family's money by way of an allowance.

And yet there were others who made their way without family help. Why he was not one of them, he wasn't sure.

He wandered down to the great hall just as Braxton opened the front door to let in a snow-drifted form. The two murmured as the footman helped the man off with his soaking greatcoat and top hat, then Braxton retreated with the articles, probably to dry them. Charles accosted the balding, bespectacled older man as he was about to head for the stairs. "Excuse me, are you the doctor?"

"I am. And who are you?" His tone was bluff and startled, his demeanor wary.

Charles thrust his hand out. "Sir Charles Blake, brother of the new Lord Simmons."

"Ah, yes, I had heard of your arrival." The doctor reciprocated, and they shook vigorously. "Albert Fitzgerald at your service, Sir Charles."

"May I . . . may I have a word with you when you are done examining the little girl?" The question startled even himself, and he could see doubt in the other man's expression. But he wouldn't retreat. He had questions and the doctor was likely to be the most impartial person he would speak to for some time.

The doctor's eyes, gray and rheumy, narrowed and he stared for a moment before saying, "Now why would you want to speak to me, I wonder? But certainly; where will I find you when I come down?"

"The library. I would be pleased to offer you some port, if you would take some with me."

"Make it a rule never to turn down another man's liquor, sir. I would be pleased to warm my bones in front of a good fire, too. And luncheon would not be amiss." He turned then and stumped up the stairs, bag in hand.

Charles retreated to the library, there to wait.

It was an hour or more before the physician wearily came in rubbing his eyes.

"Is . . . is the little girl all right?" Charles asked. He had, in the last hour, been brooding about the small hand reaching out and grasping his hair, and how that one moment changed something for him, his feelings. She was no longer an anonymous child, she was Delphine, the girl who had reached out to him. What would it feel like for Lady Simmons, whose body that small child shared for nine months, to watch her toss and moan, and know that her fate was in the hands of God? It would be pain beyond thought, beyond comprehension.

It hurt to contemplate it after just his brief encounter with Miss Delphine; for Lady Simmons it must be anguish.

"As well as she will ever be," the doctor said, slumping down in a chair.

"What do you mean?" Charles said, spilling some port into a glass and handing it to the weary man.

The doctor took a long draught, and then leaned back in the chair, the ruddy glow of the fire lighting his lined face. "Little Miss Delphine came into the world two months early, and has had to struggle ever since," he said. He shook his head, a melancholy expression on his face. "Lady Simmons was ill for the first year or so after the birth, and it was as if mother and daughter shared a fate, and that fate was to not be long in this world. I told Lord Simmons, I said, "*My lord, you are going to lose your wife.*" I said it in this very room."

"What did he say in response?"

"What could any man say? He said the will of God would be done."

Cold reaction, Charles thought, with some anger. She was his wife, not a servant or pet. His wife! Surely his reaction should have been anger, or anguish. "Nothing more?" Charles exclaimed. "That was all he said?"

The doctor shrugged. "Maybe he was thinking he could always marry again, maybe have an heir instead of a girl child. He was mighty disappointed when Miss Delphine was born."

"But neither of them died."

"No, eventually Lady Simmons got stronger, and since then I do not believe she has ever had a sick day. Weary often, discouraged, sad, but never ill. The same cannot be said for her daughter. Little Miss Delphine . . . I would never say it to her mother, but I do not believe she will live to see her teen years."

Charles felt the shock clear through to his backbone. "What? Not live?"

The doctor shrugged and set the empty glass

aside. Charles took the hint and the glass and poured more, stumping back over to the doctor and handing him the brimful vessel.

"Every time I am called up here like this," the doctor said, "I expect the worst. She had been getting stronger over the summer and autumn, even through Christmas, but now this . . . I don't know. I just don't know. This could be it."

Gloomy old sot, Charles thought. He stared into the fire and remembered the look of yearning hope on Lady Simmons's lovely face when Delphine reached out to Charles. His throat clogged and his eyes burned. He clenched his fists in his lap. "There must be something you can do?"

Braxton entered, bearing a tray with cheese, bread, tarts, and cold meats. He set it down on a sidetable and then bowed to the two men. "Shall I bring coffee, gentlemen?"

"Yes," Charles said, and as the footman exited he said to the doctor, "Please help yourself to lunch, sir. May I ask you some questions, though, as you eat?"

Remembering his own experiences with doctors as a youth, Charles questioned the doctor closely as that man cleared much of the food on the tray, and was stymied by the physician's inability to give a reason for his gloomy prognostication. Delphine had been ill often, yes, but had always recovered, and in the fall and winter had seemed to be gaining strength. His pessimism seemed to spring from this unexpected recurrence of fever, not from any actual observation.

When they parted ways, the doctor to head back to the village, Charles returned to the library and sat for a time alone, staring at the fire in thought.

* * *

"I think that despite what the doctor says, this time is different somehow," Nell said to Lundy, as she watched Delphine sleep. "She never had that rash before, those blotches." She pointed to the angry red rash on Delphine's neck and cheek. The rash was patchy and Delphine had to be kept from scratching it at times. "What do you think, Lundy?"

"I think it's too soon to tell anything." Lundy sat in the corner knitting, as always.

"I suppose."

There was silence for a moment, but then Lundy burst out, "And I think the doctor a sour old persimmon."

Nell sighed. "I did not ask your thoughts on Doctor Fitzgerald."

"I know. That has never stopped me in the past, and I don't suppose it will stop me in future. What do you think of your houseguest?"

Nell cast her maid a suspicious look, only to be confronted by the vision of innocence, and her maid's graying head bent back over her knitting. "He is hardly my houseguest, Lundy; he is here at the behest of his plaguy brother, and since this is officially Lord Simmons's estate now, it is his hospitality his brother is receiving."

"He is very well-looking, for a fellow with such a reputation," Lundy observed, squinting down at her knitting.

"You really should use glasses. Your eyes are going bad."

"My eyes are just fine, my lady."

Nell watched her struggle, then leaned over and

moved the lamp closer. Despite the fact that it was not evening yet, the light was dim, the blowing snow having obscured the window somewhat. "What would you know about Sir Charles's reputation?"

Lundy sniffed and glanced up from her work. "Well, I shouldn't say, certainly . . ."

She paused for dramatic effect, but Nell was not going to pry for more information. She was not really that interested in any gossip about Sir Charles Blake, and felt that Lundy was just trying to take her mind off her worries over Delphine and the doctor's gloomy pronouncements.

Lundy finally launched back into speech. "But it is easy enough for anyone to read between the lines of what his man Godfrey says about him and his activities in London. He does naught but gamble and drink it sounds, from morning to night."

"I should have guessed as much." Still it disappointed her. Why she should have thought there was something different about him, she couldn't say, but there had been something in his behavior toward Delphine, a softness or . . . she couldn't put her finger on what it was, but it separated him from other men in her mind. And Delphine's reaction to him was startling. But she was snatching at straws now, hope that her little girl's interest in the knight would rally her, rousing her to work to get better.

"Good-looking he is, though," Lundy observed slyly.

"I'm glad you thought so. I have never liked blond men."

"Your husband was blond."

"What hair he had left. What does preference have to do when one is to be married, though?"

"In second marriages, I am told that preference is a consideration."

Nell gave her a sharp look and retorted, "Since I will never marry again, that has little to do with me."

"Never is not in the heart's conception," Lundy observed.

"How sage you are today. And how romantical. Have you taken to reading Delphine's fairy stories?" She was being bitter and biting, but if anyone would forgive her it was Lundy.

Both were silent for a while, and Nell watched Delphine anxiously. She had tried to disregard what the doctor had said before he left, but it rang again in her ears. He had ventured to guess that her daughter's mysterious illness was progressing, just as he had predicted it would years ago. No matter what progress she made, she was doomed. Maybe not this time, but her fate was signed.

It couldn't be true. Life without Delphine . . . impossible. She wouldn't contemplate it. She shifted anxiously, squeezing her hands together, and stared at Delphine, trying to will her strength into the tiny fevered body. Having her baby and needing to get well for her had been what pulled Nell from her slough of despondency so many years before. Now Nell would return the favor and will her baby to live on, to struggle, to defeat the wraith of illness and death that loomed.

"For me, Delphine, try, darling; try for Mama." Tears welled. She could feel Lundy's anxious gaze on her.

"My lady," Lundy said, laying her knitting aside.

"Why do you not go to lie down? I would guess that you didn't have much sleep last night."

"I may," Nell said, undecided. "But if Delphine should awaken . . ."

"The doctor gave her those powders; she'll sleep peacefully for hours now."

"But if she should . . ."

"I'll find you."

Nell laid one hand on the older woman's shoulder. "I . . . I think I need a few moments," she said. "But I couldn't sleep even if I tried. You'll find me in the chapel if you need me."

SIX

Meadow House was old, probably sixteenth century, and beautiful, Charles thought, with the view of almost thirty years instead of his childhood eyes. Restless and depressed of spirits, he roamed, remembering years gone by.

He had known the house since he could remember as his grandfather's indisputable kingdom. As a child it had seemed overwhelmingly large, compared to the Blake family home, a more modest dwelling, and he had never felt as though he belonged there in any way. This had been impressed upon him by his elder cousin, Roald Blake, whose inheritance it would someday be. Roald seemed so old to him as a child, though he realized with a start that he was likely just about his own age now when Charles was ten. Even his cousins Lester and Latimer, older than he and George by just a few years, had behaved as though they were feudal lords, and he just a serf.

Both had died young, predeceased by their father, so when Roald inherited and then bore no heirs, then died, George became viscount, against all odds. It was, George often stated, the Simmons

Curse, leading to untimely deaths for all of the heirs.

If George should happen to succumb to an illness, Meadow House and the viscount's title would all be his. That thought stopped Charles for a moment, and oddly, fear clutched him. But George, despite his fancied illnesses, was as healthy as any man alive, and so careful he would never die.

Why did the thought of inheriting Meadow House and the viscountcy appall him, Charles wondered? It would be the end of all financial worries, certainly, but being viscount would bring with it a huge number of responsibilities, if one took the position seriously.

And he would take it seriously. So that was what he was afraid of, it seemed, responsibility. He didn't trust himself enough to think he could do the position— or any position—justice. He was serious enough to know he would take the responsibility seriously, and frivolous enough to fear that fact.

He wandered on, touching the wood panels, glancing at the paintings of generations of Simmons's heirs. Now, as an adult, he could admit that it was truly a lovely house. The windows were deeply recessed and diamond-paned, but the rooms had been redone some time in the last hundred years to create a warmer effect than they originally would have had. Thick carpeting and Turkish rugs covered the floors, and paper in elegant designs livened the walls. But still, the spacious rooms and paneled corridors rang with ghostly, mocking laughter, the gibes of childhood and the pain of youthful tears. His time there had always been filled with horror. As the youngest of the cousins he was the butt of many pranks, the target of many practical jokes.

As he strolled, he remembered . . . yes, there, if one knew just where to press in the paneling, was the secret staircase that led to the gallery above the ballroom. They were the same stairs his cousin Latimer had tossed him down while George laughed merrily. Latimer was dead now, drowned while swimming drunk in the Tigris River on his wedding trip many years before. Charles sauntered on, past a pair of marble columns that framed the entrance to the great hall. His cousin Lester had tied Charles to that column, leaving him there with no breeches on for all the maids to laugh at. George had shrugged and run off with Lester when their grandfather had approached. Lester was dead now, too, dying at the battle of Copenhagen, the result of a misfired cannon.

The rapid succession of deaths—all his sons had predeceased him, then his grandsons Latimer and Lester—had hastened the old Lord Simmons's passing, some had whispered, but really, the man was eighty-three when he finally died after an apoplectic fit. Charles had cynically never thought that his grandsons' deaths had affected the old man. Roald was heir anyway, by the time Charles's cousins died, and the old termagant had hopes of Roald, who favored him in so many ways, being just as cold and bad-tempered as his grandfather. And Roald was already married, with hopes that with his new young, healthy bride he would have an heir, or perhaps several, to solidify his own family line's right to the title.

But he had died without male issue, and George

had lived to inherit. Who had expected the junior branch of the family to take such root?

With the practiced pace of years, years spent perfecting a swaggering walk that masked his lameness, Charles went down a passage he didn't remember well until he was actually in it. It was a long dark corridor, unlit, cold, dank, and . . . ah, yes; he remembered now. It was the way to the chapel.

The chapel. He came to the doors, double and arched with a gothic peak and carved finials, ornate and august. On one memorable snowy night in—what would it have been 1795? . . . yes, that was one of the Christmas holidays he had spent with George at their grandfather's—miserable and alone, Charles had crept off to the chapel to avoid Lester and Latimer, only to find George there, quietly crying.

What had he been crying about?

Charles opened the chapel door, and though he didn't expect to find it so easy, the door swung without a single creak or squeal. Such a well-cared-for house! The room was cavernous and huge, but there were lighted candles on the altar and he advanced to stand at the back of the room, facing the enormous stained glass window that loomed over the alter.

When Charles accosted him, George had said he was not crying, but his pinched white face was stained with tears. And then he had said, "*Charlie, don't hate me. I can't help what Latimer and Lester do, for they're bigger than me, too, and older. I hafta go along with them.*"

Funny how he had forgotten that single, solitary

apology over the years. It came to him now that George was, cowardly but understandably, protecting himself from bullying by his more ferocious cousins by taking part in their bullying of Charles, the littlest target, and lame, besides.

The muffled echoes of sobbing interrupted his ruminations, strangely seeming a part of his past and yet of his present, too. It melted from being George's hysterical sobs to something more wrenching and heartfelt, an adult's pain and bewilderment; the sound was coming from somewhere close. As his eyes adjusted he could see a prostrate figure close to the altar, a woman's willowy form. As he watched, sheltered at the shadowy back of the chapel by the overhang of the entrance, he saw Lady Simmons lift her pale face and gaze up at the stained glass, a depiction of Jesus with the children, and she whispered, her hushed, unintelligible prayer flitting up into the vaulted heights of the chapel.

He should leave. He was intruding, and he should find some way of leaving even the house, for this was a woman sore at heart over the illness of her child. He turned, thinking he and Godfrey could at least make it down to the village to stay, surely. His presence was another burden on a woman who had too much to bear already.

But the moaning sigh of fresh sobs made him turn back.

Undecided he stood for a moment, until stillness would not answer the urgings of his conscience; then without thought he moved down the aisle as fast as his awkward gait could take him. He knelt at her side and encircled her in his arms, feeling her body tremble and quiver against him. She started and stared up at him, her tear-trails sparkling in the candlelight, and then she collapsed, sobbing bitterly against his shoulder. He held her and rocked her, murmuring words of encouragement and comfort. They sat together on the cold floor, his arms around her, her head on his shoulder.

It was a moment out of time, made sacred by their surroundings, but also by compassion on his part and surrender on hers. Utter peace enveloped him as he held her, and he gave up all doubt and cynicism, letting solace flow from his heart into hers.

Silence fell at last, and her tears stopped. She drew away from him and dabbed at her eyes with a handkerchief.

"I'm sorry, Sir Charles," she said, her head drooping. "I . . . I just . . ."

"Don't be sorry, my lady," he said, his whispered words echoing back to them. "Please, it's terribly cold in here and you're shivering. Come and revive yourself with some sherry, for you're badly in need of a restorative." He assisted her to stand, and she staggered against him.

"Ah, my foot's asleep!" she said with a rueful laugh. She patted her gray dress down over her legs and rubbed to get the feeling back. "Perhaps you're right. It has been such a long day and night. I do so apologize . . ."

"Please, don't." He put his arm around her slim shoulders. "Just come with me."

She sighed and leaned against him, and he helped her from the chapel, down the dim corridor and through the dull passages to the library, calling out to Braxton for sherry for Lady Simmons as they passed through the great hall, where the footman polished a silver urn. Charles noted the startled expression on the footman's handsome face, but he scurried off to do Charles's bidding. Settling her in a chair by the fire, he knelt awkwardly down and stirred it to life again, adding a scuttle of coal from the pail.

She glanced around. "I rarely come to this room. Too many bad associations."

Startled, he met her gaze. "You too? This was the punishment room when grandfather was alive."

"When we moved to Meadow House after Roald succeeded to the title, he did all of the ledgers here, and we would go over my household budget. From the day we wed to the day he died, he questioned every expenditure and insisted on thinking I overspent for the servants' clothes and food, and even medicine for Delphine."

"I suppose that, too, was a form of punishment," Charles said, standing by the fire, one elbow on the mantle. "To hold you so closely accountable . . . and you his wife."

Wearily she lay her head in her hand and stared at the blaze as it leapt to life. Her face was pale and drawn, still, with the circles under her eyes he had noticed earlier. But there was an added layer of hopelessness that tugged at his heart. How despondent must she have been to retreat to the chapel to weep so despairingly. And so alone.

"I spoke with Mr. Fitzgerald before he left," Charles said.

Her expression soured and hardened. She sat up straighter. "Testy old wretch. I refuse to think that he is right . . . I just refuse. I *cannot* give in to his pessimism or I'll shatter."

Charles took the chair next to hers and covered her hand with his. It startled him, the feel of her slim, cool hand under his, even though he had been the one to place it there. She shivered. "Are you cold?" he asked, pulling her shawl up over her shoulders.

"I'm always cold in this house in winter. Do you know Roald wanted me to cut back on coal for the servants' rooms? Lundy told me that often when the maids awoke there would be frost on their coverlets. I couldn't do it. I increased it instead."

He smiled, liking the indignation in her voice. "What did you do? Argue with your husband over the cost?"

"Sometimes. But finally I just took extra money out of my dress allowance."

"For the servants' coal?"

"Yes." She eyed him in confusion. "Why do you sound so surprised?"

"I just . . . I didn't think a lady would forfeit fashion."

"And who was there to see me and gape in this gloomy old . . . this house." She looked swiftly away.

He hesitated, but curiosity got the better of him. "Do you not love this house?"

"Of course I do," she said.

He wasn't convinced, but set aside his conjectures for later, when he was alone. "About Delphine . . ."

She turned her hand and clasped his. "Thank you for telling her your story," she said.

He squeezed her chilly hand, trying to infuse her with his warmth. "I was touched when she . . . when she grasped my hair. No child has ever taken to me like that."

"Your hair," she said, reaching up and touching it. She smoothed it back, twisting the locks in her fingers.

He felt a shiver course down his back and took a deep gulp of air, combating the urge to pull her close again, as he had in the chapel.

"She saw the sunlight on it," she continued, unaware of his impulse, "and it reminded her of the Gilded Knight in the garden, I think. Just because of its golden color, you see."

"In the garden? I understood 'The Gilded Knight' referred to a fairy story."

"It is, but out in the garden . . . I don't know if you remember, but there's an old statue of a knight on a horse, the horse pawing the air. The knight is St. George, I think," she said, then gave a self-conscious laugh, perhaps because of the name. "He's wearing armor but no helmet."

"I don't remember it."

"It's Delphine's favorite statue of all of them. The . . . the day before she fell ill she was out there, and the ice had crusted it. As the sun began to set it lit the statue up until it looked like gold. She was entranced . . . said it was the Gilded Knight from the story." She sighed and her smile died on her lips. "I should have seen the signs and not even let her go outside, for now I see she was already beginning to get feverish." She pulled her hand away and covered her face. "I should have seen," she said, her voice muffled. "I shouldn't have let her stay out so long."

He pulled her hands down.

Before he could say anything, she blurted out, staring into his eyes, "What if the doctor is right? Oh, God, what if he's right? I can't lose her, I just can't!"

"Stop! You said yourself he is gloomy by nature." He swallowed hard. "Lady Simmons . . ."

"Don't call me that! Anything but that!"

He paused, nonplused by the anguish in her voice and the bitter expression on her face. "I . . . don't know what to call you then."

She glanced at the fire. "My given name is Nellwyn."

"It's lovely."

"It is said that someone in our family was related to the infamous Nell Gwyn," she said, with a slight crooked smile. "But the less scandalous history of my name is that I had Welsh forebears. One girl in every generation is given my name."

"I suppose our relation and acquaintance is of long enough duration to allow me to call you . . . Nell?"

"You could call me Cousin Nell," she said, biting her lip.

It was impossible to resist. He liked her. He liked her very much and it made things impossibly complicated. He grinned. "You *are* my senior; I should be respectful."

"By a year or so," she retorted. "That's not so very much!" Their raillery had made her forget her troubles for a moment, but then her smile died and her expression sobered.

"You know," he said, in a rush. "Doctors said when I was born that I wouldn't live."

"Really?"

He had caught her full attention with that conversational gambit. "Yes. I was . . . was born . . ." God, this was hard, but he pushed ahead. "I was born lame.

Though both of his sons were a disappointment to our father, I was more than a mere disappointment like poor Georgy, I was . . . repulsive in some way, I suppose." He shook off the melancholy with determination. "But that is neither here nor there. What I started to say was that the doctor did not expect me to live. And when I thwarted his gloomy prognostications by making it first one day, then two, he predicted, my mother told me, that I would never walk. But I did. And then when I fell ill, he predicted that even if I recovered I would be blind, for it was some kind of fever. He was wrong about that, too."

She took a deep breath. "I see what you're trying to do, Charles, but medical science has come so far in the last thirty years, we know so much more now . . ."

"But your doctor is sixty years old at least. Does he even know of recent medical advances?"

"I don't know."

"Or does he cling to the old ways? And even if he does know, when have doctors been infallible? Every generation has its advances and still, people live who doctors predicted would die. I swear they are a gloomy hopeless lot. I lived in spite of my doctor, not because of him. He dosed me with emetics and potions, leeched me and cupped me . . . it was a wonder I had any blood left to pound through my veins."

When he met her eyes it was to see faint hope dawning there, like sunlight in a blue sky. "He's been predicting her death since the day she was born, but she always lives, and until recently, was getting stronger!"

"This may be a brief setback, but she will get better

again, Nell, you have to believe that. If she was getting stronger before this, you have to believe she can overcome again."

"Yes; I'll try to believe. I *will* believe!"

"Good! It has been a very difficult year for the poor child. Losing her father . . . no matter what, it cannot have been easy for either of you."

"It was such a setback for her when Roald died," Nell said. "I don't understand it, because he never paid her much attention. Why did she care so much when he died?"

"He was still her father. It's a hard blow to a child, I suppose. I was old enough when my father died that I felt only resentment." He hadn't meant to sound embittered, but was afraid his tone revealed too much, for she gazed into his eyes with a searching expression. Having never said such a thing to anyone, he was rather shocked with himself, but she wasn't, he could see it.

"Why do fathers have so much trouble showing love to their children?" she asked.

It was an idle question, he thought, and not one she expected an answer to. He didn't have one, anyway. "What is little Delphine like?" he asked instead. "She's my cousin . . . I should know these things."

Nell smiled. "She's like sunshine to me. Bright and happy most of the time, sunny and sweet and lovely. You can't tell right now because she's ill, but she's . . . joyful, lively."

"Are you angry that she took it so hard when her father died?"

"I could never be angry with her!" Nell cried. "Never!"

But when she thought about it, she wondered.

Had Charles struck on something? Was she angry that Nell was so crushed by Roald's death, when she, his wife, only felt a vague relief? Shocking. It was shocking to even consider it. She pushed the thought away and instead pondered Charles's other assertion, that Mr. Fitzgerald, old and stuck in his antiquated ways, had no idea how to treat Delphine and so had given up on her.

Had she doomed her own child by her stubbornness in staying in Gloucestershire and Meadow House?

Braxton brought in sherry and served, then disappeared, and Charles handed her a glass. She downed the warm liquid in one long swallow, seeking warmth against the persistent chill that had invaded her bones.

"You're still cold," Charles said, taking her hand.

She nodded and he refilled her glass.

"We're so far from the fire," he said. "Come, sit down here. You need the warmth right now."

"No, it's all right, I . . ."

"Come! I'll brook no refusal, you know. Just do as I say."

He took her free hand and pulled her down to sit by the hearth. At first she felt awkward. The only time she ever sat down on the floor or ground was when playing with Delphine. But staring into the fire, letting the warmth seep into her bones, she began to relax, and then the pressure of his hand on her back rubbing in slow circles, lulled her into a trance.

"You must take care of yourself, Nell," he said, gently. "I can see you are exhausted, and you will do your daughter no good if you come down ill, too."

True, she thought. He continued rubbing, and she began to feel drowsy, the sleepless night telling, finally, and the sherry taking its effect too. She rested against his shoulder. He was not a big man, but he felt solid and comfortable. She drained her glass and he took it from her hand and set it aside.

"Close your eyes for a moment," he murmured.

"No . . . no, I should be getting back up to Delphine." She tried to rouse herself, but he kept her there by the fire, and she stopped resisting.

"She's sleeping, likely," Charles said, "The servants know where you are, and your maid will take care of her. She seems a sensible woman."

"Lundy is more than sensible. She saved my life when I was ill after having Delphine."

"Then the child is in good hands. And so is her mother. Rest, Nell."

His hands moved again to her back and massaged. She closed her eyes and drifted hazily.

"Come, lean against me and close your eyes for just a minute."

Relaxing back against his shoulder, she closed her eyes again. When she felt soft lips against hers, she opened her eyes and stiffened, gazing into his eyes with alarm, but he murmured against her mouth, and kissed her so tenderly that she surrendered to how unexpectedly sweet the caress was. Her eyes drifted closed, the kiss deepened, and she hazily felt that she ought to pull away. But he was very good at it, and she had not been kissed in so long . . . years. Many years. And never like this, never with this lazy sweetness.

She sighed, but her comfortable mood was interrupted by the sound of someone clearing his throat somewhere above her. She opened her eyes and gazed up at Braxton, who stood stiffly over her.

"My lady, Miss Lundy requests your presence. Miss Delphine is ill, vomiting, I believe, and breaking out."

Charles scrambled awkwardly to his feet and pulled her up. She snatched her hand away from him and glared, but then turned her attention back to the footman. "I shall be there momentarily," she said, feeling the shame burn in her cheeks.

When Braxton exited she turned to Charles and said, shaking with agitation, "You took advantage of me, sir, and I'm ashamed for both of us. Please leave Meadow House. You can see that with Delphine ill we cannot leave at present, even if I wanted to."

He stared at her for a moment, but then said, "I'm afraid, Nell, that I must echo some of your words." He limped over to the large draped window and pulled the curtain aside. It was a blizzard of white outside the glass, even the upper pane coated with blowing snow. "I'm stranded here for now, so you will just have to put up with me."

SEVEN

As angry and cold as Nell was, still, as she left, she took with her all the warmth the room had had for him. Charles stood by the window, staring at the door; he touched his lips with one hand and wondered what had just happened and why he had kissed her like that.

It was indescribable, the feeling that overcame him when she relaxed against his chest, surrendering to his hand at her back, which was only meant to warm her. He had looked down at her, her sweet pink lips pursed, and want conquered sense. It was beyond reason, and yet his mind would race, trying to define it, attempting to understand it. He had wanted to surround her in warmth, cradle her in safety. He longed to ease her worries and soothe her aching heart.

What was wrong with him?

He trudged from the library and up to his own suite. Godfrey, meticulously neat and proper as always, spectacles on his nose, was in the dressing room working at a stain in Charles's trousers with a damp cloth and a bottle of spirits.

Charles, unwilling to be alone even if it meant resorting to the company of the one man in the world

who knew him as well as he knew himself—or perhaps better—sagged down on the settee near the
door to his bedchamber and watched his valet work.
He had never been the kind for affairs of the heart,
though he had placated his carnal desires with affairs
of the flesh on occasion. Actresses were pleasant and
complaisant, and didn't expect much but the occasional gift and rewards for fidelity. An exchange of
benefits like that he understood, but he didn't understand his urge to kiss Lady Simmons . . . Nell.

He looked up to find Godfrey watching him,
paused with a cloth in one hand and the trousers in
the other.

"I'm beginning to think that I have taken on an impossible task," Charles said. "The poor child is really
ill. I can't ask Lady Simmons to take her daughter
away from here when she's unwell. Can I?"

The valet studied him for a moment over his
spectacles, used only for close work, then said, "Failure means your brother will have no compunction
about letting you be cast out of your lodgings, with
the duns after you."

"I know, I know!" Charles threaded his fingers
through his thick thatch of hair and leaned back in
his chair, cradling his head in his woven fingers.
"How did I ever let myself get into this mess?"

"You won't stop gambling and your income is
not sufficient to allow you to both gamble and
lose. When you lose you have not the money to
pay your debts, and so you take money from your
allowance when it is meant for rent and food and
servants' wages."

Giving Godfrey a sour look at his too-literal answer, Charles resumed his train of thought. How

had the kissing started? He had invited Nell to sit down closer to the fire because she was so cold, and then he had begun massaging her back to try to warm her. He had no other intention then but to erase her weariness. He had just discovered how much he liked her, and though frightened by that revelation, he was intrigued, too.

As he felt her relax, her body sagging against him, he had felt a surge of some undefined emotion . . . some desire to hold her and protect her. How ridiculous! How could he ever protect her? Her life was beyond his sphere of influence.

But she didn't know that. She might think he had more influence with George than he really did, and she didn't know about his deal with George to get her out of Meadow House in return for enough money to settle his debts and start clean in London. The more he thought of it, the more likely it seemed that she was trying to subtly persuade him to intercede on her behalf with George.

Why did she need that intercession, though? All she had to do was comply. She had been stalling for long enough. What kept her in the damned house anyway?

Godfrey shook out the trousers, folded them over a chair, and took up a jacket, examining a tear under the arm. He sighed and shook his head, but began work on a stain on the pocket first.

"Lady Simmons thinks I won't press for her to leave," Charles said, sitting up in his chair. "But it is George's home, dammit! He has every right to expect her to leave. And she has a house in London, an income . . . what more could she want?"

"A well child?"

"Godfrey, continue with your work and don't be impertinent, or I'll give you the sack."

Eyebrows raised, the valet glanced up at his employer, the glass of his spectacles sparkling in the lamplight. "Oh, that would be terrible," he said, in a heavily ironic tone. "I would not have an income then. What would I do?"

Charles glared at him. His valet had not been paid his quarter's wage yet, and the next quarter's was due. "You do your living on me, Godfrey. If you are so unhappy, you are free to find other employment."

The valet shrugged. "You happen to suit me, sir. Don't know why."

Charles wondered on that topic for a moment—why did Godfrey put up with him?—but abandoned it in favor of the nettle that continued to sting him, the question of why Nell refused to leave Meadow House. "As I was saying, this is my brother's house." He gave the valet a sharp look, but the fellow just nodded and bent back over his work. "And I cannot help but feel that Lady Simmons is using this illness of her daughter's as a way of prolonging their stay."

He did not need Godfrey's incredulous look to let him know that it was a ridiculous statement. Saying it out loud had made that plain even to himself.

"I know," he said, in answer to Godfrey's unspoken criticism. "That is . . . despicable to say. And I don't really think it is true."

"Then why did you say it?" Godfrey said, pausing in his work.

"Who are you to question me?" Charles shot back. Sometimes Godfrey really did go too far. He might just have to sack him one day.

But no, he would never do that. He wouldn't

know how to go about finding someone else to suit. And in fact, Godfrey's question was the same one he had just been asking himself, so out loud he tried to find the answer. "Why *did* I say that? Why do I keep trying to justify what I came here to do?" He shook his head. "I don't know. Guilt? Godfrey, I just found Lady Simmons alone and crying in the chapel a while ago, and had to help her back to the library and give her a restorative." Pensively, he stared down at his hands, clasping his knees. "I wanted to help her, make it all go away, all the pain she is going through, all her little girl's suffering."

He pondered that while Godfrey continued his work, patiently wiping at a greasy spot on the jacket sleeve. "What if the poor child should die? How would Lady Simmons go on?"

"Women have always had to bear the deaths of their children, and often their men too," Godfrey said, quietly. "My own mother buried seven children before dying while giving birth to me. I lived, by some miracle, and was sent away."

"My mother lost a baby before I was born. I was her last. Father told me he wouldn't touch her after I was born." The bitterness in his voice surprised him, made him think.

"Sir Charles," Godfrey said. "Take it from one older than you by many years; you must let go of past injustices and past pain if you are ever to move on in life."

"So speaks the broken-down valet attached to a wastrel younger son who gained his knighthood by . . ." He stopped. He never spoke of the deed if he could help it.

The valet set aside his glasses, shook out the

cleaned jacket, and crossed to the clothespress. Charles watched him, realizing he had just insulted the man on purpose, and that was not like him.

"Sorry about that 'broken-down' part," Charles said. "That was unfair."

"No apology necessary, sir. You should know that by now."

Godfrey had been a steady part of his life for years, and rarely complained. Charles had always had a sense that Godfrey had a secret past, perhaps the reason he was content to work for Charles when a fellow of his undeniable ability and steadiness should have had his pick of aristocratic masters.

Returning to the subject that would not let him alone, Charles said, "For a few moments, while I was able to comfort Lady Simmons, I felt like . . . I felt like a man, a *whole* man, one with something to offer." And it had frightened him. He had been, if he was truthful, almost relieved when she had accused him of taking advantage of her. Her bile had released him from some feeling of responsibility, if only temporarily. It was back full force now, the wish that he could protect her from anything that was yet to come. Was that how other men felt about their wives and daughters?

He rose and limped over to the window, pulling back the curtain and gazing out at the blustery dullness of the day. Snow still beat against the windowpane and the sky was a sheet of leaden gray. He turned back to tell Godfrey that they were stuck there for a while at least by the weather, but his valet was staring at him with an odd look on his face.

"What is it? You look like you've been 'smacked with a question stick,' as my nanny used to say."

"Why do you think, sir, that you are not a whole man? Or that you've nothing to offer?"

"Don't be absurd!" Charles blurted, taken aback. "You know all my secrets, damn you, and you know what I am. Even on the exterior I am just a lame younger son with no money and a worthless title. Dig underneath that glossy finish and you'll find the refuse pile of life."

Godfrey paused, pressing his lips into a firm line, but then said, "I have witnessed, in society, a number of uneven matches that society said were all benefit on one side and yet . . . I always knew that there was more than one kind of benefit. Money will never replace a dying child, nor will it ever fill the void left by a lack of care . . . a lack of . . . of love in one's life."

"Godfrey, the poetical valet," Charles snorted. "To think I have known you all this time and never knew you were a romantic at heart."

The fellow turned away and continued his duties. But over his shoulder he said, "Deflect what I say as you will, there is truth in my words, and I think you know it. It's why you're so frightened. No one has ever expected or needed anything from you. The thought that you have something worth giving is as frightening as it is novel."

Charles had no answer, and wasn't sure he understood what Godfrey was saying. There was silence for a few minutes as he stared out at the gloom and his valet continued his unhurried work, retrieving a mending kit for the jacket and donning his spectacles once again.

"How ill do you think the little girl is?" Charles said.

"I don't know, sir, I'm sure. What does the doctor say?"

"I don't believe in doctors," Charles barked, his voice harsh in the hushed room. He patted his thigh with one hand and thought, then said, "Will you find out what you can from the staff, Godfrey? I . . . I need to know how long her recovery will take if I am to know what to tell George."

"I doubt if any mail will get through to your brother for some days, at least, sir."

"I know, I know! Just find out what you can. You ought to love this; I'm asking you to gossip and chat and flirt with the maids, if need be. Are you not good at all of those things?"

"Every valet is good at flirting with the maids," Godfrey said, his tone light. He bit off the thread as he finished his mending, hung up the jacket, and closed the clothespress. "So, is this information I am to retrieve all to further the ambition of getting Lady Simmons to leave Meadow House, Sir Charles?"

"Of course. What other reason could I have?"

"Indeed."

Wringing out a cloth, Nell laid it on Delphine's forehead, but her child tossed it away; she thrashed and whimpered.

"Too bright," she whined, pushing away the covers.

"What is it, darling?" Nell asked leaning over the bed. "I don't understand."

Delphine put one thin hand over her eyes. "The light . . . it's too bright, Mama."

The day was dull but there was only one candle lit in the room, and it was away from the bedside.

Feeling a shiver of apprehension, Nell knew that this sensitivity to light was a new symptom, one Delphine had never exhibited before.

Martha dithered into the room with a fresh bowl of water, putting it down on the table with a clunk. Some sloshed over the edge. In normal circumstances she was a steady young woman, but for some reason with this bout, she was nervous and agitated, little help at all to Nell or Lundy.

"Why don't you go down to the kitchen and get me some tea, Martha," Nell said, as Delphine moaned and whimpered, thrashing and pushing away the covers again, even as Nell tried to keep her covered.

With one frightened look at her charge, Martha curtseyed and obeyed. Nell vowed to get to the bottom of her agitation, but it would have to wait until Delphine was better. Whenever that should be.

Lundy quietly entered. She silently went about tidying the room, and brought the bowl of fresh water to Nell. There was clearly something the woman wanted to say, but she was holding back.

Nell sat back in her chair as Delphine settled with the cooler cloth on her forehead. "What is it, Lundy? You clearly have something on your mind."

Lundy sat on the low stool and looked up at Nell with concern in her tired eyes. "I was just speaking with Mrs. Howard. She told me . . . it seems that young Willie, the potboy, is feverish too. He came down with it yesterday, he thinks, but didn't tell anyone until he collapsed as he was scrubbing."

Shocked at the news, Nell covered her heart with one hand and said, "That's terrible! Poor child. Where is he?"

"Mrs. Howard put him to bed in his room. But she asked if you would look at him for her. She's concerned about the fever."

"Fever. Hmm." Nell glanced at Delphine, who had quieted considerably.

"I'll stay with our darling," Lundy said, putting one small hand on the covered form.

Nell touched Lundy's shoulder, no words needed to express her gratitude, and swiftly left the room. She almost raced down the hall and mounted some very steep steps to the true attic, which was above only the oldest part of the house. One part of it was turned over to servants' bedrooms while the rest was storage. When she had come to Meadow House, the servants' quarters had been so drafty and poorly glazed that snow blew in through the cracks. She had been appalled, and in those first few years after Roald's succession, when her husband had still been moderately fond of her and had hopes for an heir, she had been able to convince him to allow carpenters to repair the walls. She had the rooms painted and had old linens from the family chambers made over for the beds.

She found the appropriate room, one Willie shared with the stable boy and gardener's helper, and entered.

Martha was by the bed, but started away guiltily when Nell entered. "I-I know I'm supposed to be gettin' your tea, ma'am, but I just . . . I just came to check on Willie . . ."

"This is your brother, isn't it? I had forgotten until this moment."

The girl, white-faced, nodded, then burst into tears. Nell hushed her with one hand on her arm, and said, "You mustn't break down. Willie will need you if he is ill." She knelt by the bed. The boy was just eleven and slight of frame, with a thick thatch of rusty hair that drooped in his eyes. She pushed it back and laid her hand on his forehead. "He is very warm." She stared at him in the dim light of the window. "And he has some blotching, I think. Martha, get a bowl of cool water, as you did for me earlier for Delphine, and a clean cloth. I cannot be in two places at once, and so if you would like, you can take care of your brother while Lundy and I care for Delphine."

Tears in her eyes, the girl nodded jerkily and then turned and exited.

"Don't take too long," Nell called after her.

Alone with the child in the dimly lit attic, she watched him thrash and whimper. He was trying to say something, and she got closer to make it out. "What is it, Willie? What are you trying to say?"

He put one hand over his eyes. "Light's too bright."

That was what Delphine was complaining about. Exactly. And it was something her daughter had never said before in all her bouts of illness. What did it mean?

Martha came back with the bowl of water and a stack of clean rags. Nell dipped one in the water and laid it over the boy's forehead. "This is what you must do for your brother, Martha, just as we have been doing for Delphine. Stay with him," she said, rising and giving over her spot to the nursemaid, "and keep a cool cloth on his forehead. I'll send up a pitcher of water and a glass. Try to get him to take some water, too. Fever must be combated with liquids. He may not wish to eat, and he must not be forced, but water he should have."

The girl nodded and then leaned over her brother. Nell watched for a moment.

"Martha," she said, puzzling things out in her head. "Did Willie and Delphine ever come in contact with each other?"

"Oh, no, ma'am, no, I . . ." Martha stopped and burst into tears, shivering and sobbing.

Nell knelt by her and put one hand on her shoulder. "Martha, just tell me the truth."

The nursemaid nodded, weeping and sniffling, her eyes red and swollen. She wiped hastily at her eyes and squeezed them shut, quelling her tears with a supreme effort. With a long, deep breath, she shivered and sighed, then said, more calmly, "M-miss Delphine and me were outside, an' Willie come out, and he stopped to talk to me, and the two began playing this game Miss Delphine had learned, from Miss Lundy, I think. She taught Willie and they played for a half hour, and . . . and . . ." She burst into tears again. "I'm so sorry, ma'am, and now . . ."

"Martha, stop! You must be strong and care for your brother." Nell sat down for a moment on the end of Willie's low bed, puzzling things out. "When was this?"

"Must be . . . three days ago, ma'am? Four? 'Twas the day before the icy fog, ma'am, so that would have been Tuesday, four days ago."

Hope and fear warred in Nell's bosom. This new fever and illness, then, might be just an infectious disease like all children were prone to. When she was young she had had many and survived after an uncomfortable few days.

But on the other hand, Delphine was more fragile; would this new challenge be the death of her?
It wouldn't, she vowed it to herself.

She rose. "Martha, I think we have some infectious illness here. What that means is that we must
try not to infect others in the household, and more
especially not let it spread. In that respect the
weather is fortunate, for we'll have no deliveries
nor mail for a few days. Stay with your brother and
I will have lunch and tea sent up for you. But the
maid will only leave it at the door. I want as little
contact as possible between those who have certainly been in contact with Willie and Delphine,
and those who have not. It is likely too late, but
there is still a hope we can confine the illness. We'll
just be as careful as we can."

"Yes'm." Martha said. "Will . . . will my brother be
all right, ma'am?"

"He's a healthy boy, Martha; I'm sure he will be."
She only hoped she could say the same for her own
child, her baby girl, Nell thought.

She returned to Delphine's room to tell Lundy
what she had discovered. When she was done, she
said, "And Sir Charles must be told, too. For he was
up here with Delphine, and she touched him. He
could be infected."

"Wouldn't do him a bit of harm to be brought
down with a fever," Lundy said, "but I suppose he
must be warned. You should tell him, my lady.
Miss Delphine is sleeping peacefully. Why don't
you go now?"

"I suppose I must," Nell said, reluctantly, thinking of how she had left him, and wondering what
had come over her. Though she had accused him

of taking advantage of her, she couldn't imagine how she had let herself be lulled into such a state that she had acquiesced, or worse, participated in the kisses.

But there was no getting around it; she must see him again. Of all things she was not a coward, though there were many things she would have preferred to face than the man she had just kissed so recently. She would just pretend nothing had happened, and hope that he would go along with the charade. That was her only recourse, especially since she couldn't explain any of what happened.

Her greatest fear was that he understood it all too well. Understood and would try to take advantage of her tumultuous feelings.

EIGHT

"Where is Sir Charles?" Nell asked of Braxton, the footman, as she descended the last two steps to the great hall. She was determined that even with he who saw her in the knight's arms, she would pretend nothing had happened. Her staff were not gossips . . . she hoped.

He looked up from the work he was directing the junior footman to, a tarnish spot on the brass planter that flanked the staircase. "He is in the billiards room, my lady."

His expression was as impassive as usual, his tone cool, and she was satisfied. There would be no further embarrassments—being caught by her staff in a compromising position was certainly an embarrassment—and all would return to normal. Straightening her dress skirts, she strode toward the billiards room. It had not been used for years, and she only glanced at it occasionally to make sure it was all in order, but when she entered she was struck by how different it seemed with an occupant, warmer somehow. Enlivened. A masculine room with a masculine presence. Sir Charles was bent over the table making a difficult shot, and she stayed still until he took it, then entered.

He looked up and nodded a greeting. "My lady. I hope you don't mind that I have made myself at home here."

"Why would I mind?" she asked, standing some feet distant from him and clasping her hands together in front of her. His blond locks were tumbled over his forehead from his last shot and she had an absurd urge to smooth them back. His arms around her, his lips pressed to hers: those sensations kept coming back to her. "I-it is more your home than mine. It is your brother's property now, after all."

"Ah, you concede that, anyway." He took another shot and missed.

"I have never argued that. I'm no simpleton." His casual demeanor was irritating to her, with her feelings so raw, and she felt like grabbing the cue stick and throwing it away. She could picture grasping it and throwing it like a javelin, right through the window. It would soar out over the hedge and onto the grass beyond. It was a most satisfying image and she took vicarious gratification from it. Still clutching her hands in front of her she said, "I only wish to stay here through the full period of my mourning. That would take me to the middle of April."

"Are you so sorry old Roald is gone?" When she was silent, he looked up from his shot and straightened. "I'm sorry, that was disrespectful and rude."

His apology was more startling to her than his rudeness. Roald had never apologized, no matter how cruel he was to her. "It *was* rude," she said, though, giving him no quarter. "Why are you here, Sir Charles? Why did George send you and why did you come?"

"I already told you of George's peculiarities."

"But that doesn't explain to me why you acquiesced. You seem unhappy to be here."

He shrugged and continued playing.

Irritated by his nonchalance, she circled the room and pulled the curtains aside, gazing out at the snow.

"I've never seen weather like this," she said, idly. She glanced back at him and he took a shot, managing a difficult one around an interfering ball, banking his shot off the side of the table.

He was so at ease, she wanted to shake him and ask him if he always kissed vulnerable widows like he did. And did he always do it with such matchless skill and sweetness? And did he always make them want to go on and on, forgetting that they had an ill child and a duty to be done? She despised his ease, and, wanting to rattle him, she said, "I came in to tell you, Sir Charles, that even if the weather improved we would not be able to leave. It appears that we have an infectious breakout here."

He missed his stroke and tossed the stick down with an exclamation. "What do you mean?" He stared at her, his forehead wrinkled.

"I mean exactly what I say," she said, enjoying his discomfiture. "Willie, the potboy, is exhibiting symptoms like Delphine's, and was in contact with my child, too. It appears that we have two cases of some infectious fever, and will have to quarantine the house for a time. I must ask you, since you were with Delphine, to comply with any rules I put in place to limit the spread of the disease."

"I am surely exempt, Nell. I have only been here a day!"

"However, you touched Delphine and she is likely

contagious. I'm afraid I must insist, Charles. " She was taking too much delight in his unease; what did that say for her disposition?

He frowned, but then said, as he moved toward her, "All right. It seems everything, even the weather is conspiring to make me stay. If I believed in such things I would say that fate is scheming to keep me here . . . with you."

How neatly he had turned the tables. She backed away from him as he advanced on her. He made her uneasy and she didn't know why, but given her recent behavior he might just think her vulnerable to his charms. She hadn't even figured out why she had let him kiss her, nor why she couldn't be angry about it even now, despite her accusation that he was taking advantage of her.

He stopped finally, and stood at one end of the table. "How is Delphine doing?" he asked, rolling one of the billiard balls toward the others. They connected with a clacking sound that echoed.

"She's uncomfortable." Nell caught one of the balls and picked it up, rolling it around in her hand. "I am hopeful though . . . if it's just a childhood illness, then maybe . . . maybe the recovery will not take so long as it has in past." She frowned and looked down at the colored ball. "Maybe. I have hope, at least." Perhaps, she suddenly thought, her preoccupation with Charles and his kisses was just her own mind trying to keep from worrying about Delphine. That made no sense to her logic, but it was better than any of the alternative theories . . . like she really had enjoyed his kisses and caresses, or that she enjoyed having someone to lean on and someone to take care of her.

That would never do. She had never had that before and getting used to it was unthinkable.

Holding himself back with all the strength he could summon, Charles saw the worry in her lovely eyes, and the pain, and if he thought he could have soothed her, he would have damned all caution and taken her in his arms again. But judging by her outburst earlier it only made matters worse.

His stomach roiling at the tension of wanting to hold her again and needing to control that urge, he said, "Every child goes through such illnesses. I would say if you have brought her through more serious times, she will recover from this."

"I'm praying you're right."

"Do you play?" he asked, pointing at the table and picking up his cue stick.

"I used to." She put down the ball and rolled it to the middle of the table.

"Show me."

"Good God," she exclaimed, drawing herself up in indignation. "I don't have time for a game! If you have forgotten, I have an ill child . . . *two* ill children . . ."

"Who are both in good hands." He organized the balls on the table. "Five minutes. Show me you do more than tend to others."

She pursed her lips and glared at him, but when he merely smiled back, she took a cue stick from the rack on the wall and leaned over the table, knocking the balls and sending them skidding across the felt.

"Very bad!"

"I said it had been a while," she retorted.

"What do you do with your time here at Meadow

House?" He took a shot and sent one ball neatly into a corner pocket. "You take a shot now. We'll just take turns. I'm not playing to win."

She narrowed her eyes and gazed at him for a moment, no doubt trying to decide if he meant what he said or what he implied. She then frowned, bent, and took a shot that was better than the last, but still resulted in nothing more than balls hitting each other. "I look after Delphine, take care of the house, do the accounts, consult with the land steward."

He stifled his too swift enjoyment of the view of her bent over the table. It was really wrong to be thinking of her thus, though she was a remarkably pretty woman. "No, I mean, what do you do for enjoyment?" He took a shot and sent another ball into a pocket, then sedately chalked his stick.

"I . . . well, I visit. The vicar has a society that I belong to, and we do . . . do good works. And . . ."

"No, for enjoyment," he insisted, standing his stick up against the table and moving toward her. He steadied her arm and showed her a better position for her hand on the stick, and then helped her stroke the ball gently into the pocket, enjoying too much the feel of her rounded bottom pressed to his trouser front.

She laid her stick down then and moved away from him toward the door. "I . . . I have enjoyment."

She was as skittish as a fawn, he thought, his own heart pounding at the nearness of her, and her warm scent. In that moment, molded against her, helping her take her shot, his blood had heated like pitch in a cauldron, and his mouth was dry.

But something about their closeness was frightening her, and he wasn't sure if she sensed his own longing, or if she was feeling something herself. She was pale and a nerve jumped near her eye, and he was ashamed to again be thinking things he ought not. He tamped down his potent urges and thought about her. She was scared for her child, and her emotions were raw and close to the surface, judging by her weepiness earlier and her defensiveness whenever they spoke of Meadow House. Whatever she was thinking or feeling in this moment was as much the product of that awful disquietude as any real emotion.

That sensible thinking cooled him. "Have you eaten anything today?" he asked.

"I . . . yes, I had breakfast, I think."

"That was some time ago. Nell, you cannot ignore your own well-being, if only for Delphine's sake. Have some supper with me."

"Delphine . . ."

"Go check on her, but if she's sleeping, or if she appears all right, leave your maid with her and come have supper. Not in the dining room; I dislike that room. In the morning parlor."

"The morning parlor?"

He shrugged. "It is, at least, cheerful and not as vast as the dining room."

Reluctantly, she agreed, and said, "I'll go and check on Delphine. But if she needs me, or if . . ."

"Then you must stay with her, of course," he said, gently. "Meet me in the library, and then we'll go have some supper."

A half hour later, to his surprise, she joined him in the library and they moved together, his hand under her arm, through the great hall to the morning parlor, where a small table by the window had been set for two. The blaze in the hearth was already taking the chill from the room, and as Charles seated Nell, Braxton and another footman brought in the covered plates and set them down on a narrow table near the door.

"You can see I made free with the household," Charles said. "I hope you don't mind."

"It is . . . odd to be taken care of in my own home," she said. But she smiled to soften her words.

"So I must assume Delphine is sleeping peacefully."

"She is for the moment. She was awake when I went in, but as I spoke to Lundy she drifted off. She's still fevered, but is calm. I am told Willie is much the same."

"Willie is . . . the other infected child?"

"Yes, the potboy. He is Martha the nursemaid's brother."

Braxton and the other footman served, but only Braxton stayed, standing near the door. Charles watched Nell eat, and could tell her mind was still upstairs with her daughter. How would that be, he wondered, to have someone whose well-being was one's responsibility, and more, one's dearest concern? He had never had to look after anyone but himself, and he hadn't done such a good job of that, judging by his financial difficulties and wasted life so far. He stared at the window, but with the day darkening beyond it, it acted more as a mirror than as a window. He did not want to gaze at his own reflection. To avoid further contemplation, he resumed their conversation. "I must assume, Nell, that Meadow House is very dear to you, if you wish to stay."

Pausing with a fork full of chicken, she said, with a startled look, "I am mostly concerned for Delphine, you know. She likes it here."

"Pardon me, but would she not like it anywhere you took her? Children are portable, you know."

Nell, not meeting his eyes, said, "I just say what I feel. I will leave when I feel it's right. I don't think it's too much to ask to stay until April. Is your brother so impatient?"

"Not so impatient, but I think he feels that he does not possess the full dignity of his title until he can possess the house and estate too."

"Then he should have come himself."

"I told you about his fears. He's consumed with worries about his health. Another reason why he wants to leave London."

"And another reason why I don't want to go to London! If it is unhealthy for a man, consider how it will be for Delphine!"

"Really, Nell, if you are going to use George's irrationality as your own yardstick, it is a poor measure. And anyway, Dorsey House is in Chelsea. I can tell you, that is a most healthful part of London, and most beautiful, with lovely gardens and the embankment to walk daily. If I had a house in Chelsea, I would never leave it."

She ate some more, ignoring his gentle chiding. "I didn't realize how hungry I was," she said, with a chagrined smile. "Where do you live, Charles? With George?"

"Good God, no!" Charles shuddered. "No, I have rented rooms."

"And what do you do with your time? It's a fair question, since you asked me earlier."

He shrugged carelessly. "What does any man do?"

She looked up then, and he was startled by the glimmer of laughter in the sky blue of her eyes. "Oh, is *that* what you do in London?"

"What do you mean?"

"Chase actresses, drink, and gamble too much."

"Why do you say that?" he asked, uncomfortably aware of how much that described his life.

"I have a brother . . . *had* a brother." She turned sober. "Tony did that, until he bought a commission and joined Wellington on the Peninsula. He died there. I wish he had just kept chasing actresses!"

Charles watched the happy light die from her eyes. He lifted his glass and held it up in the candlelight. "I propose a toast to all of the good men who have lost their lives, to Tony, and my friend Roger, and to all the other gallants chasing Nappy around the continent. Would that I were one of them."

She was arrested in the act of raising her glass. "You? What do you mean?"

He confessed then his dream of joining the army when he was younger, and his father's refusal to buy his commission. "Then I came here. It was just about two years before grandfather's death—and a year before my father's—and I . . . I asked him to buy my commission."

"What did he say?" she asked, putting down her glass.

Charles felt again the pain and disappointment. And the humiliation. "He said the army did not need lame soldiers." He twirled his glass by its stem and the wine sloshed around the bowl. "That I would only be a liability, and would get myself and my men killed. He said I wasn't worth the cost of the commission, for it would be throwing it away."

"Oh, Charles!" She reached over and put her hand on his. "I'm so sorry. How hurt you must have been."

"I was young. If he had just bought me my colors, I would have forgiven him all the other . . . all the years of taunts. Instead, I celebrated when he died soon after, a few months after my father died. I drank to his death. That was wrong."

"But you were very young and very hurt."

Charles took a long, cleansing breath. "It is why, when George and I came to visit after Roald came into the title, and after you had Delphine, I stayed drunk the whole week. It was the memories, the feelings . . . I was not good for anything for a while."

She sat back, folded her hands on her lap and gazed down at them. "I was not at my best then, myself. I was ill for so long after Delphine was born. Doctor Fitzgerald thought I would die. If it wasn't for Lundy, I probably would have."

"That's your maid?"

"She is much more than that. I almost died, Delphine has almost died several times; if not for Lundy, I would not have been able to manage."

"The entire staff here adores you, you know, and that is much more rare than you may know. Respect is the most one can expect or ask for from people who see us at our worst so much of the time. Is that why you stay? Do you love it here so very much?" To his shock, tears started in her eyes. It was his turn to reach out, and he put his hand on her arm. "Nell, what is it?"

She shook her head.

He left his seat and knelt at her side, wiping one tear from the corner of her eye. "Tell me."

Her brow furrowed, she muttered, "I can't. You will think me an idiot."

"No, I promise you I won't. What is it?"

Her voice low, she said, "When I was young, I went to the harvest fair at the village near my home, and this . . . this gypsy fortune teller, she looked at my palm and said . . . oh this is stupid!"

"She said 'oh, this is stupid'?"

"No!" Nell smiled against the glimmer of tears and turned in her seat to gaze down at him. "How can you make me smile? This is important."

"Then tell me," he said, gently, taking her hand and squeezing it.

"The fortune teller told me I would only have one true home in my life, and that every other place would bring me misfortune and sadness. I . . . I'm afraid to leave here; isn't that idiotic?"

"Nell, have you been so fortunate and happy here, then?"

"Well . . . no, but . . ."

"Then, even if it were true—and I don't believe in fortune tellers, though many people do—even if it were true, how do you know that your one true home is not waiting for you in London or somewhere else, and you won't find it until you leave here?"

NINE

Nell stuttered and gazed down into Charles's brown eyes. "M-maybe you're right. I hadn't thought of that." She stared at his face, the honest emotion in his expression, the intelligence of his open gaze, and doubted what she was seeing and feeling. He appeared to care, but she must keep in mind that his stated purpose in being at Meadow House was to get her to leave at the first possible moment. His conjecture could be a part of that.

And yet, what he said had merit.

"It's just a thought." He squeezed her hand one more time and released it, then stood.

"I'm normally so sensible; I can't say why that old prediction stayed with me all these years, but when Delphine was a baby I was so happy . . . I love her so much." She shrugged. "It made me fear I would lose her, I think, if I left here, where she was born. It may sound ridiculous . . ." She stood, too, finding his height above her distracting. "Thank you for . . ." She waved a hand around, indicating the room and the dinner. Perhaps it was preposterous to thank him for her own home and food, but never had anyone outside of house staff cared for her well-being. It was an odd feeling, but not entirely unwelcome. "I have to go back up to Delphine now."

Charles watched her go and was surprised by a powerful urge to follow her. Warmth had seeped into every corner of his being as they ate and talked together, and for a moment he had imagined that this was how marriage was. And yet for the married men he knew—and he knew many—a night at home was to be avoided at all costs and in any way. The wives had their circles of friends and the husbands theirs, and they occasionally were forced to go together to balls or dinner parties, though they would seldom leave together. However he only knew how they lived when in London. When they were at their country estates perhaps they dined like this, intimately by the fire.

Maybe. Or maybe they led their separate lives in the country too. But that was their choice, whatever they did. Certainly if he had a choice and a wife like Nell, he would dine with her every night, and then take her off to bed.

On that improper and scandalous—but stimulating—thought, he moved back to the library and sat with a postprandial glass of port. Inevitably boredom set in, though, when he was faced with his own thoughts and worries. Anything was preferable to that. He had already inquired as to the possibility of going down to the village that evening, but was met with a stolid no, the roads were not passable, and indeed had gotten much worse since the doctor's visit. And the house was quarantined, even if it was possible. He had to remember that.

His mind drifted back to the child, and how her eyes had lit up when she saw him. Perhaps he ought to go up and see her again. And maybe Nell would be there.

He was on his way before he had time to doubt his decision.

The upper reaches of the house were still and dim. He would be intruding perhaps; he should go back. But there was nothing to go back to.

He listened outside the door for a moment and heard voices, or at least one voice. He rapped gently and then entered, standing just inside the door. Nell was not there. A little woman, the maid named Lundy, likely, was the only occupant of the room other than the child in the bed, and it appeared that she was reading a storybook out loud.

"I . . . I thought perhaps my little cousin might like a visitor," he said, hesitating, and wishing he had not heeded his idiotic urge. "How is she?"

The maid's expression, while not unfriendly, was not welcoming either. "Feverish still, but comfortable. Lady Simmons is up visiting Willie, if you're wondering."

So she saw through his charade, when he hadn't even allowed himself that honesty of vision. He stepped forward. "I did come to see little Miss Delphine."

At that moment the child shifted on the bed and opened her eyes. In the dim light Charles could see her expression and it warmed him, how she brightened, her eyes focusing and her smile lifting the corners of her mouth.

"You came to see me!" She reached out one hand. "Sit by me? Please?" She turned and gazed at the maid, her expression perfectly lucid. "Lundy, may he?"

But Charles wasn't waiting for the maid's approval. He moved over to the bed and sat down on the edge of it as Lundy moved away to a chair where a pile of gray knitting indicated her usual occupation. Delphine was . . . how old? She must be nine, he supposed, as he examined her, but to his eye she seemed so frail and small. Not that he was a judge of children's ages and sizes, but shouldn't she be more robust?

She squirmed to get comfortable and he helped her, pulling the blankets up to her chest. She pushed them away, but he gave her a look. "You have to keep these covers up, Miss Delphine, or I promise, I shall leave."

She acquiesced and sighed, snuggling down.

Italy, he thought suddenly; that was the place one took invalids to recover. If he was her father he would take her on a sea voyage to Italy, where the warm sun and the sea air, the good food and interesting scenes would give her natural color and add pounds on her thin frame. When the girl reached out her hand, it was the most natural thing in the world to take it, cradling it in his own, marveling at how small it was, slim fairy fingers nestled in his broad palm, white against the healthy pink of his hand.

"I thought you were a dream," she said, her reedy voice lifting with a humorous lilt. Two bright spots of feverish color burned high on her cheeks, but she was lucid and smiling. "I often have interesting dreams."

"No, I'm as solid as a pork pie," he said, gently squeezing her hand in his own. He pinched his own arm and yelped, then grimaced. "See? Quite real. Shall I pinch you now to prove it?"

"No," she said, and giggled. "Are you really a knight, or was that part a dream? I'm often not sure right now; Mama says it's because of the fever."

"I am indeed a knight. Do you remember me telling you all about how I became a knight?"

She nodded, staring up at him. "But tell me again?"

How could he resist? It was one area of his life that had only, after the first few heady months, given him shame to reflect upon, and yet if it made her happy he was willing to tell the tale again and again.

Looking up once he caught the steady, calculating gaze of the little maid—she was a tiny woman, not more than a child's height—and was aware for a moment that she was for some reason judging him. He was not accustomed to that kind of impertinence except from Godfrey, but he didn't quail under her watchful stare.

When he was done the tale, he could see that Delphine was getting sleepy. She had let go of his hand and as her eyes closed her lashes drifted down, fanning her cheeks; then she opened her eyes wide, trying to stay awake.

"Don't fight it, my little friend," he said, softly. "My little cousin. We *are* cousins, you know, family."

She smiled drowsily, yawned and closed her eyes. He reached out, but stopped, hesitant, and gave the maid a quick look. Her expression was stolid, but he would not be intimidated by a fierce little maid. He touched Delphine's cheek and felt her forehead, smoothed back her hair. It was damp. "Go to sleep, now," he said, with the gentlest tone he had ever used.

"Will you come back to see me?" she murmured.

"Of course," he said. "I'll come back tomorrow, if you like."

She nodded, her eyes still closed. "Please."

"I will. And tomorrow I'll tell you a new story, about how a clever little boy, Charlie Blake, fooled his cousins and his brother and found the best hiding place in all of Meadow House. And you can tell me if you can guess the hiding spot."

She was asleep.

The door behind him opened and Nell came in just then. He put one finger to his lips and indicated Delphine, sleeping peacefully with a sweet smile on her lips.

He won a prize, a smile on Nell's face that echoed the child's and rivaled it for sweetness. His stomach lurched. It was time to leave and go to his own bed. Not to sleep, he supposed, but to read or think, neither being activities he was accustomed to.

Nell noted a sudden agitation in Charles, and he exited quickly, with just a nod and hasty "Good night" for her.

When the door closed behind him she sat down on the edge of the bed and watched Delphine sleep for a moment.

"How is Willie?" Lundy asked, her voice a whisper.

"Better. Still feverish, but Martha is a good nurse, better than I thought she was; he was lucid while I was there. What did Sir Charles want?"

"To see you," Lundy said, but then added, "though he *said* he wanted to see how Miss Delphine was."

"Then we will assume he was telling the truth," Nell said, frostily. "And how did they fare?"

With a grudging tone Lundy said, "The child was

happy to see him. He told her the story of his knighting again."

"Did he say this time what he did to earn it?"

"No."

"Surely one would think it was part of the story," Nell mused, smoothing the bedcover. She was silent for a while, and then turned to Lundy, "Why don't you go down and get your supper? And send Adele to make up my cot. I'll be sleeping here again."

Once Lundy had left, Nell thought for a while about her "guest." He confused her. She supposed in a way he was a welcome diversion from her worries, but he also left her perplexed as to his true intentions, and flustered by his presence.

In truth she had no intention of leaving Meadow House until she wanted to, but she was beginning to think that would be the moment Delphine was well enough to travel. She wouldn't say that to Charles, though. Let him think her plans unchanged.

There had been a time when Delphine was young that she had wanted to take her to London to see what physicians there would say about her recurring fever. Roald had firmly said "no," and she had come to believe it was best for her daughter to stay in the country. But now the world was opening up to her again, and if they could just get past this illness she would be glad to move on, explore life, make a new home for herself and Delphine. After all, what had she ever found at Meadow House but pain and illness, all under the disapproving eye of her husband?

The future had to hold something better than that. And even if she did have Dorsey House, there was no reason she had to live there. She could lease it out and travel, or move anywhere. They could go to the seaside, if it turned out that was best for Delphine's health, to Lyme Regis or Wight. Roald had not been a good husband in many ways, but he had not left her poor, and she blessed his memory for the surprising income he had thought to provide her with. Maybe he did care for his daughter.

For the first time she thought beyond tomorrow, beyond Meadow House, beyond life as she had been living it. Without a grand country estate to care for, she would have free time. What would she do with that time?

She stared into the dark and wondered.

Charles did not return to the lower floor when he left Delphine's room, though. He remembered vaguely . . . he moved down the dimly lit hall and found what he was looking for, more steps, even narrower, up into an old attic in the original old part of the house, which had been built in stages as much as two hundred years apart.

Treading softly, he picked up a lantern from a table and moved up the steps to the narrow hall of the old attic. His foot was beginning to ache, but he determined to ignore it. He limped down the hall, noting the neatly made beds he could see through open doors. Servants' quarters up here, certainly, for kitchen staff and outdoor workers, but if he remembered right there was a storage area too.

He saw a low door at the end of the hall, not even adult height, and he moved quietly toward it. Was it locked? He turned the knob and tested it with his weight. It was unlocked, giving at his push, and he ducked under the lintel and crept into the storage space.

It was cold and dusty, with festoons of cobwebs hanging like festive garlands from the rafters. His opening of the door caused a swirl of movement, as if he was disturbing long-dead ghosts. The lantern cast weird shadows, those behind him being of his own elongated body. This indeed was the place he had thought of when he spoke to Delphine of hiding places, for he had hidden from Lester and Latimer many times, until they had complained to their grandfather about it and the old man had told him that it was unmanly to hide from his cousins in that cowardly manner. And so he had not hidden, staying instead to receive the beatings they thought his due.

He glanced around him. There was a wealth of old furniture, some ghastly and Jacobean, heavy and cast aside for the lighter profiles of the current fashion. Some merely with broken legs, like racehorses put out to pasture. He climbed past the furniture and found a dressmaker's form and several old trunks lined up against one slanted wall. Most of the trunks were locked, likely against servants' predations; his family was a suspicious lot.

But there was one with no latch on it, a smaller and simpler one that he recognized. It was made of rough, unfinished wood and had tin corners and hinges, rusting to reddish brown. He knelt by it, remembering it from days gone by. It was where he hid his things when he was trying to evade notice from his cousins and brother. His paintings. Yes, and his art supplies, for his cousins loved to torment him about his love of drawing.

Lester in particular was ferocious about destroying any painting he caught his younger cousin at.

Charles set the lantern on a larger trunk nearby and opened the small, unlocked cask. There was an old jacket on top, dusty as he pulled it out and laid it aside. And yes . . . some art supplies, old squeezed-out paints, brushes, papers, and a couple of canvases. His mother had encouraged his painting before she died. She loved art herself, though she never said so in front of her husband.

Sitting down on the floor awkwardly cross-legged, Charles pulled the paintings and drawings out and put them in his lap. He moved a little closer to the lamp and looked them over.

There was a poor rendition of a dog; or maybe it was a rabbit. Impossible to tell.

And a portrait of his Nanny Lowell; it looked a little like her. She had died the year he graduated school and he had cried, as sad as when his mother died. He traced the line of her pouchy chin. She had loved him with no reservations and had let everyone know it. It wasn't just the love that touched his heart then, but the courage she displayed before she was retired, pensioned off against her wishes.

He leafed through more paintings, a few poor seascapes; since he had never seen the sea at that age he had no conception of its appearance except from other paintings. And then . . . yes, he remembered now. He *well* remembered; how could he have forgotten?

He gazed down at the picture of the statue, the green tints of the foliage around it indicating its place in the Elizabethan knot garden. It was of a knight on a horse, the horse rampant and the chevalier waving his sword in the air, his flowing locks streaming out behind his unhelmeted head.

The Gilded Knight.

TEN

As odd as it seemed even to himself, Charles was anxious for morning. He had the painting of the statue by his bedside and longed to show it to Delphine; it was an unexpected connection between them, a coincidence that they should both have such a strong feeling for the old statue.

He had rescued all his paintings and drawings from the old trunk, and when morning came he sat on his bed and looked them over in the light of day. They were a ragged lot, stained and curled at the edges, and the renditions were no better than they were by lamplight, but he had been happy while he drew and painted, and so each one held fond memories.

"What are those, sir?" Godfrey said, as he entered the room with a tray for Charles. Acting as his employer's personal servant was one way, he told Charles, of keeping on the good side of the staff and making a favorable impression, by not adding to their daily work.

Charles spread out the canvases and watercolor sketches on his bed. "I remembered these from my childhood visits here," he said, and explained his early predilection for painting and drawing. He pointed to the one of the statue. "That happens to be little Delphine's favorite statue out in the garden."

"The Gilded Knight, sir?"

Charles looked up at him. "How do you know about that?"

Giving him a withering look, Godfrey said, "Serving staff know everything." He gazed at the watercolor and then at his employer. "I would think that is rather good for a child."

"Not really. But recognizable, and that's why I want to show it to Delphine."

"You like the little girl, sir."

"I . . . I suppose I do." He paused and stared down at the painting, pondering his feeling of connection to his cousin, but then he shrugged. "How can one not like a child? Perhaps if she was racing around pulling things down and making a nuisance of herself I might not like her, but she's confined to bed, a quiet little thing. Maybe that's the charm." He stared at the painting for another moment. Now he remembered his work that day, how he had sat on a low rock wall nearby in the sun and painted, until George came out and threw a stone at him. He had thrown a stone back, of course, and had broken a window, if he remembered rightly.

After that he was chased down by the gardener and marched in to his grandfather, who had taken away his paints and locked them up somewhere. The attic, it appeared, or perhaps the attic trunk came later. And then he was whipped, as usual.

But if he remembered rightly, George was also punished that day by having his favorite pony taken away from him, so he couldn't ride, and being whipped as well for his part in starting the

fracas. Charles hadn't considered until that moment that for every awful memory he had of his
cousins and grandfather, George might have one
just as horrendous.

Something to reflect on.

He drank his early coffee and then shuffled the
paintings into a pile and rescued the art supplies,
some charcoal and putty, pencils, and paper, from
the table near the window. Still in his dressing gown
he crept down the hall, up the stairs, down the
third-floor hall, and up the narrow stairs to the servants' chambers. As early as it seemed to him, he
knew that all of the staff would be already at their
work. Except one.

He found a modest room with one occupant, a
young boy who lay on his bed staring up at the
frosted window. When Charles entered he sat up
and stared, two spots of high color on his cheeks.

"Who are you?" the child said.

"A friend," Charles replied. He approached the
bed and sat down on the edge. "You must be Willie;
am I right?"

The child nodded, staring up at the apparition of
a gent in a satin dressing gown.

"Don't be frightened, Willie; I am Sir Charles,
Miss Delphine's cousin who is staying here. I heard
that you were ill, too, and I thought that you might
be bored and lonely, so I brought you this." Charles
spilled the pile onto the bed, and then worried at
how pitiful it might seem, some used charcoal and
pencils, a stack of drawing paper. He knelt down
and spread it out. "It . . . it's for you to draw, to
while away the time. I was ill often as a child, and
drawing helped me pass the time. Draw whatever

you like; trees, horses, houses. I'll find some picture books for you to draw from, if you like."

Willie just stared at him, and Charles felt a little the fool. The impulsive gesture was probably the last thing the boy needed, but perhaps it would help him pass some time. He stood.

"Anyway, try drawing something. It helps pass that time away when you can't get out and run and play . . ." At the last minute he realized the child didn't really run and play, he worked. He shut his mouth. His own life of privilege seemed very soft to him at that moment, and he vowed never to complain about life again, not when there were children working for their living. He knew the philosophy; the lower classes did not feel things as keenly as the aristocrats. They were not born with finer feelings. Work was the only thing that kept them moral and humble.

In that moment, in that dim attic room, he didn't believe it. A twelve-year-old boy was a child, but this child worked. It was a humbling thought.

"I hope you're better soon, Willie." He turned and walked to the door.

"Sir?"

He turned. "Yes?"

"Would you come again, sir? Please?"

"I will. And I'll bring you a picture book."

"With dragons in it, sir? I've heard of dragons, but . . . but I've had a powerful hard time thinkin' what they'd look like."

"I'll see what I can do."

He slipped out and back down to his room, powerfully moved and touched. The spark that had twinkled in the boy's eyes would remain with him for some time to come.

After breakfast, he tucked his painting of the statue in the garden under his arm and headed back upstairs. He traveled the familiar route to Delphine's room, and tapped on the door.

Nell was there, and she smiled and let him in.

"How is she this morning?"

"The same," Nell said, on a sigh.

When he approached the bed, Charles was disappointed to find that Delphine was sleeping. Uncertainly, he set the painting down and turned back to Nell.

"What is that?" she asked, looking over his shoulder.

"It's . . . it's for Delphine."

She was staring down at it. "Where did you get that from? That's . . . isn't that the statue out in the garden?"

He picked it up and sat down, holding it close to him. She sat down on the low stool by Delphine's bed.

"I had forgotten about this," he said, holding the picture out and gazing down at it. He met Nell's wondering stare. "When I was here one summer, I brought with me the paints and pencils my mother had given me for my birthday. I drew a lot, and painted some. I had forgotten until last night . . . I went up to the attic and found these in a trunk. This is mine," he said, holding up the painting. "I don't know why I didn't remember the statue until I saw this, but time does odd things to the memory. I suppose we remember what we want. Anyway, this is the last thing I ever painted, I think." He looked down at it. "I was sitting on the garden wall; you can tell from the angle. It's not very good . . ."

Delphine murmured and stretched.

Nell, her eyes sparkling, stood and leaned over her daughter. "You have a visitor, darling," she said, then straightened and moved to the door. "I'll be back in a little while." She quietly exited.

Delphine was subdued and listless, but she smiled when Charles showed her the painting and seemed pleased. It was not the happy reaction he had anticipated, and to his own eyes she seemed not better than the day before nor even the same, but a little worse, perhaps, less energetic, more languid. They visited for a while, she drifted to sleep, but as he was about to leave and find her maid, she opened her eyes again.

"May I keep the painting for a while?" she murmured. "It looks like summer."

"Certainly," he said, and propped it up at the end of her bed so she could see it when next she awoke. "Sleep well, Delphine," he said.

Lundy entered just then and he muttered a farewell and retreated to the library downstairs.

The next few days took on a pattern, Charles noted. The weather had closed in to such an extent that they were housebound. There was no mail, no newspapers, no communication with the world beyond the borders of Meadow House land.

But the estate was self-sufficient, with laying hens and milk cows, and stores of vegetables and preserves enough to last months. It was a curious suspended state of affairs. Charles, exploring some of the old forgotten recesses of the house, felt an odd sense of nostalgia for Lester, Latimer, and George. Even George. Until he remembered the extortion his brother exercised in sending him there to oust a widow and her invalid child.

And his own destitution that made him acquiesce.

Once or twice a day he would go up to visit Delphine, and he visited Willie again, taking him an old book he had found in the library, one that detailed the legends of dragons and had a few old woodcuts to prove their existence. As the boy recovered somewhat from what had been discovered by the housekeeper, Mrs. Howard, to be scarlatina, a mild form of scarlet fever, Charles discovered that he was an intelligent and lively lad. He clearly enjoyed the attention and liked drawing, showing no latent talent at all but boundless enthusiasm, but he was soon chafing to get out of bed, even if it meant a return to his kitchen duties.

Nell decreed, though, that he was not to work for the time being. He was, instead, set to the task of learning his numbers, with his sister as his sometimes tutor. Happily, it appeared that no one else in the house would be stricken with the fever.

But Delphine was not recovering at a happy rate. Though the patchy rash disappeared at last, Charles could see how the fever still burned and exhausted her, her frail frame becoming pitifully thinner. Often she didn't have the strength to talk, and so just listened while he told expurgated stories of his youthful visits to Meadow House. In his stories the torment he suffered at the hands of Lester and Latimer became youthful pranks, little more than high spirits and boyish rowdiness. And he rarely referred to his grandfather at all.

Though Delphine listened more than talked, she still insisted on keeping the painting of the knight at the end of her bed, and was fretful if it was set aside.

He saw, on those visits, how her daughter's illness was wearing Nell down, the worry of it and the fear. He saw often the yearning hope if Delphine seemed a little better, and the shadow of apprehension if she had a bad spell. He didn't know if Nell was avoiding him or not, but there were no more dinners together, nor any accidental meetings.

Which was a pity, because he had found her unexpectedly attractive. He brooded on whether she had been frightened off by his friendly behavior toward her, but could come to no conclusion, finally. It was selfishness that made it a concern, he decided, because she had much more important things to think about than his comfort and his feelings toward her.

Idly playing cards alone at the table by the window in his suite one afternoon, a week and a few days after arriving, he frowned down at the cards at last and tossed them aside.

"Godfrey," he said to his valet, who was brushing down Charles's best beaver hat.

"Yes?"

"What do you make of this household?"

The valet stopped and squinted, his glasses perched on his nose. He looked over them at his employer. "In what way, sir?"

"Anything. How it is run, who is really in charge . . . how the serving staff feel about my brother's imminent arrival as viscount."

Godfrey, as always, went to the most interesting question first. "They are curious, I know, about your brother. They have been asking me—not outright, mind, but in roundabout ways—what I know about the new Lord Simmons."

"And what have you told them?" Charles gazed steadily at his valet. It was a view into belowstairs life that he had never had before, and he saw his valet now as a kind of personage among the Meadow House staff, sought after and feted for the knowledge he bore.

"I have thought it best to say little, sir."

Charles laughed out loud and rose from his chair. "That serves two purposes, doesn't it?"

"Sir?"

"Fraud. I see what you are doing. You are increasing their curiosity and hinting at knowledge. It never does to tell all one knows without some tradeoff." Charles threw himself down on the bed and put his hands behind his head.

Suppressing a smile, Godfrey sighed and said, "Alas, I do let the odd tidbit slip. I assured them of his moral character. Not like the rogue who is my employer."

"Godfrey! What have you implied about me?"

"Nothing, sir. Your own exemplary behavior while you have been here has won their good opinion, for the most part."

Charles sat up. His valet had never been taciturn, certainly, but this loquacity was interesting. He seemed happier himself, content in ways Charles had never seen. "Who in particular among the staff are we discussing."

Godfrey brushed the hat a few strokes. "Miss Lundy, though she seems most stiff at times—she is an upper servant and so doesn't mix freely with the other staff, but seems to feel that I am her equal—

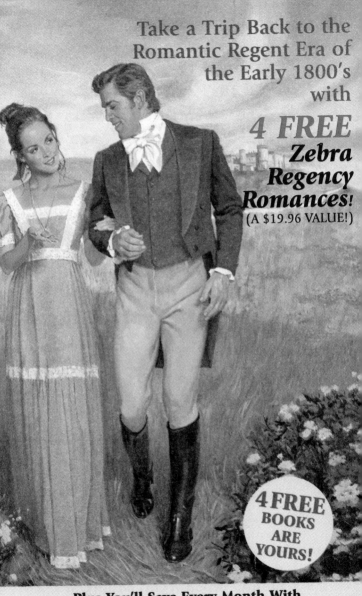

We'd Like to Invite You to Subscribe to Zebra's Regency Romance Book Club and Send You 4 Free Books as Your Introduction! (Worth $19.96!)

If you're a Regency lover, imagine the joy of getting 4 FREE Zebra Regency Romances and then the chance to have these lovely stories delivered to your home each month at the lowest price available! Well, that's our offer to you and here's how you benefit by becoming a Regency Romance subscriber:

- *4 FREE Introductory Regency Romances are delivered to your doorstep (you only pay for shipping & handling)*

- *4 BRAND NEW Regencies are then delivered each month (usually before they're available in bookstores)*

- *Subscribers save almost $4.00 off the cover price every month*

- *You also receive a FREE monthly newsletter, which features author profiles, discounts, subscriber benefits, book previews and more*

- *There's no risks or obligations…in other words, you can cancel whenever you wish with no questions asked*

Join the thousands of readers who enjoy the savings and convenience offered to Regency Romance subscribers. After your initial introductory shipment, you'll receive 4 brand-new Zebra Regency Romances each month to examine for 10 days. Then, if you decide to keep the books, you pay the preferred subscriber's price, plus shipping and handling.

It's a no-lose proposition, so return the FREE BOOK CERTIFICATE today!

IIﻪﻪIﻪﻪﻪﻪIIﻪﻪﻪﻪﻪIﻪﻪﻪﻪﻪﻪIﻪﻪﻪﻪﻪﻪﻪIﻪﻪﻪIﻪﻪﻪﻪﻪIﻪﻪﻪﻪIﻪﻪﻪIIﻪﻪI

REGENCY ROMANCE BOOK CLUB
Zebra Home Subscription Service, Inc.
P.O. Box 5214
Clifton NJ 07015-5214

PLACE
STAMP
HERE

has unbent enough to say she has appreciated your treatment of the little girl. There may have been a tear in her eye when she said it."

"Really! And I have been thinking she disapproves of my visits."

"Quite the contrary. And Miss Martha, Miss Delphine's nursemaid, was amazed by your condescension in visiting her little brother. And very touched by your gift of art materials. She . . . thinks very much of you; in fact, you are something of a demigod to her right now."

Charles watched Godfrey's face and was caught by the faint pinkening of his cheeks. "So, do I have Miss Martha to thank for your improved mood and increased verbosity? Is she the fancy of the moment?"

His valet looked shocked and disapproving. "Sir, I would not like to hear Miss Martha's name bandied about with such jocularity. She is a well-mannered young lady."

Charles was silent. He watched as Godfrey resumed his task, and then finally set the hat aside. "I believe you really do have a liking for the girl."

"Sir Charles," the valet said, eyeing him sternly. "I meant what I said. Miss Martha is a good girl, very pleasant to me, but she is so young! Only twenty-two, I believe."

More uneven matches were made every day in his world, Charles thought, but what opportunity did the serving class have to marry, even if there happened to be love? "And how old are you?"

"I believe I am thirty-four."

"You don't know for sure?"

"I know the year of my birth, but since I was a foundling, no one is sure of the exact date. The orphanage thought it must have been January or

February of the year, though. So I could be thirty-four or thirty-five at this moment."

An orphanage. How little Charles knew about Godfrey, though he had been his manservant for seven years. For such a close relationship, there was little of that information exchanged. And yet Godfrey knew every detail of his own birth and formative years because he complained so incessantly. It was not unusual, certainly, for who among his friends knew more than he about their valet?

But now he was curious.

"What would you do if you had money? Say you won a lottery tomorrow, a substantial sum, what would you do?" He sat up cross-legged on his bed while Godfrey set aside his spectacles and put the hat back in the cupboard.

Godfrey shrugged as he closed the cupboard door. "I don't know that I've ever thought of that," he said, turning to face Charles.

"Yes, you have. It would not be human to not imagine such things."

Sitting on a chair by the dressing table, the valet, his capable hands still for the moment, said, "I suppose, sir, that I would purchase a tidy little establishment in the village I was born in. When I was a lad I worked in one such establishment, the Lucky Duck; I was only potboy, but the host was as jovial a fellow as I have ever met, and very kind to me. All the villagers came for more than his fine ale, I can tell you. He told me true happiness was being independent."

Running an inn was not an ambition Charles would have imagined for his tidy, quiet manservant.

"Why did you come to London, then, and seek employment as a valet?"

He shrugged. "One needs a certain amount of capital to purchase such an establishment. I thought I might be able to find work and save money, but . . ."

Godfrey had not been paid in months, Charles thought, nor had Charles's landlady back in London. And these people had no brother to go to, to beg for money. When he did not pay them, they suffered. Was that a way for any of them to live?

Reproach at every turn. He sighed. This was turning out to be a most illuminating period of rustication.

Nell sat by Delphine's bed and reflected on the week. It had brought revelations, certainly, among them the knowledge that her staff would go on after she left Meadow House and would form working relationships with the new master and his brother, and life would continue for the estate. Had she held on to Meadow House in part because she felt that the estate would suffer if she left? She hoped that was not true, for it didn't reflect well on her own conceit.

That revelation, that the house and estate would go on and survive, had come when she realized how much the staff liked having Charles there. So too they would accept the new Lord Simmons. It was best for everyone if he was allowed to take over his birthright as soon as possible, before planning for the spring planting was begun. It was pure selfishness on her part to impede the natural flow of life, the succession of the estate to the proper heir.

She could wish that she had behaved differently in the past and moved to London in September, but she still was not leaving until Delphine was better. She would not risk her child's health for any reason.

Lundy quietly entered, back from her supper. She resumed her usual seat in the corner and took up her knitting. "Have you eaten, yet, my lady?"

"No."

"You must eat. Go. I'll watch the child."

"Not yet. Lundy, have I done the right thing, keeping Delphine here, or have I hurt her?"

"I don't think you've hurt her. Don't be starting to think that way. You've done what you thought right, and that's all a parent can do."

"I suppose." She mused as she watched her maid's needles working rapidly in another of the endless gray worksocks Lundy delighted in making. "Any new gossip about Sir Charles or his mysterious manservant?"

Lundy's beady eyes sparkled in the lamplight. "Indeed! Mr. Godfrey said that he has never seen his master in such a thoughtful mood as since he came here. He said that the gentleman seems to be rethinking his life, even though he has been a rake and a wastrel. You know, there is no man so attentive and commendable as a reformed rake."

Nell bit her lip to keep from laughing. "How would you know that particular piece of information, Lundy?"

"Why, it's common knowledge, ma'am." Lundy looked shocked at any doubt being expressed.

"What is the extent of his rakishness?" Nell asked. Though he had kissed her with disarming expertise, Charles Blake did not strike her as a rake.

"Why, he is known to drink too much."

"Mhmm?"

"And gamble. Very bad, that. I do not approve of young men who gamble."

"Nor do I. But most of them do it, I am told, despite our disapproval. Anything more?"

"Why . . . I don't know."

"Any actresses in his keeping? Any babies from the wrong side of the blanket?"

Lundy dropped her knitting and gasped. "My lady! I'm shocked, I am . . ." She gaped, though her mouth kept moving.

"Genuinely speechless." Nell again suppressed a smile. It was unladylike to speak of bastard children, and she would never do so except in front of her trusted maid. "I'm sorry, Lundy; I couldn't resist. I have always thought of rakishness as having to do with conquests rather than drink or gambling. Perhaps I'm wrong."

"You certainly are. I'm sure the young gentleman has never done such a dishonorable thing as . . . as . . ."

"I never thought you a prude, Lundy. And I'm amazed at your complete capitulation to Sir Charles's charm. You know why he is here."

Lundy nodded. "And I think you know, my lady, that I have long been of the opinion we should be in London even now."

"That's true," Nell said on a sigh. "I should have known you would see Sir Charles's mission in a different light than I."

"He is only doing what his brother has asked him to. That speaks well of his family feeling, if you ask me."

"I didn't, but when has that ever stopped you?"

The maid picked up her knitting and resumed, squinting in the pale lamplight.

"Use your glasses, Lundy. That is why I got them for you." Nell stood and stretched, her cramped muscles crying out at her for sitting too long in one position. She needed food and she needed some exercise. Maybe on the morrow she would go for a walk outside so she could tell Delphine what her favorite statue looked like. "I think I will take your advice and seek out some dinner."

The big house was quiet and empty. A long time ago she had thought to fill its halls with children and laughter. Once she had been young and full of hope, hope that her grim-faced suitor would be softened by the love he claimed to feel for her. But Roald had only become more grim, especially after she recovered from her illness, and it appeared that she was not fated to have any more children.

The house was cold. Where should she take dinner? The dining room was too big and formal; Charles was right about that.

Had he taken his evening meal, she wondered?

On an impulse she turned and headed for the library, pushing open the door to feel a surge of warm air gush out and envelope her.

"Nell," Charles said, from his seat by the fire.

"Charles," Nell said in answer, and paused, hesitant on the threshold of the room.

He stood and put down his book.

"Don't let me interrupt you," she said, ready to back out of the room.

"No, Nell, you are a most welcome interruption.

I'm dying of boredom, in truth, for I never was over-fond of books. I was my schoolmaster's despair."

"Have you had dinner yet?" she asked, on a sudden whim.

"No. Have you?"

"No. I was . . . just going to find some."

"Have it here, with me, by the fire," he said with a winning smile, gesturing to the blaze in the hearth.

Should she? Given her odd vulnerability to his unexpected charm, should she risk it?

ELEVEN

"I will," she said, suddenly sure it was what she wanted to do. Her life was ruled by duty. For once it would be overtaken by her own desires. And right now she wanted to sit by a warm fire and have someone cater to her. There was nobody better at that than Charles Blake, she had learned, to her surprise. It was disconcerting how he often anticipated her desires and fulfilled them; it bespoke a consideration she was accustomed to expressing herself, but not receiving in kind.

"Then sit," he said, taking her hand and guiding her to a chair. "You look worn to the nub, as my old Nanny Lowell used to say." He found a lap robe and laid it over her legs, as if he could calculate every chill, every shiver, and knew how to combat it. "Cook promised me a very nice roasted squab this evening," he added, "and I would be happy to share it with you."

Share it with her? "Pardon me," she exclaimed, tucking the robe in around her legs. "But am I not still the mistress here? This may be by rights your brother's house, but the food and . . ."

He grinned down at her, his brown eyes warm with laughter, and she saw he was having her on.

Her heart thudded at his handsome smile. She was so unaccustomed to teasing she had not even recognized it. She shook her head and said, "I'm not used to someone with your humor, Charles."

"I'm so overcome with the joy of talking to another human, that I am giddy, you see." He cleared away the table between the two chairs in front of the fire. "We shall have a cozy supper, and I'll try to get my fill of conversation." He rang the bell, Braxton entered, and Charles murmured to him.

To her surprise it seemed that even Braxton's resentment of Charles's high-handedness—she had heard all about it from Lundy—had melted away. The young footman's change of heart must be mere pragmatism, she thought, for he must know he would stay with the estate and that impressing the new viscount's brother was a good way to ensure his continued employment. Or it could just be that Charles had such a naturally winning way that no one was proof against his charm.

She had found herself far too susceptible to the enveloping warmth of his personality.

In ten minutes she had a glass of mulled wine in her hand, and in twenty a small table was pulled up in front of her and a covered dish placed there. She watched Charles as he made everything comfortable, and added more coal to the fire.

He stopped fussing finally, and removed the cover from her dish, then sat down to his own dinner. She was hungry, though she hadn't thought she was, and they ate for a few moments in silence, but as her immediate hunger was sated, she watched him. She remembered him from that last time he visited, many years before. She was ill, as was Delphine, but Roald forced her to take part in some activities with their guests, including dinner. She couldn't eat and had felt an odd sympathy for Charles as he was then, without appetite too, obviously nursing a headache brought on by too much wine.

She had seen no sign during his time with them now that he indulged in excessive alcohol though. Perhaps his youthful follies were behind him.

"What were you reading when I came in?" she asked, to start a conversation.

He took a drink and then said, "There is not much of interest in this library to read, since I am not one to enjoy agricultural treatises or dry relations of the Trojan War."

"But you were reading."

He shrugged. "I was forced to read a text on trade opportunities in the new world as opposed to Indian trade."

"That sounds very dry." She took another bite of her dinner and watched him. He seemed uncomfortable with her line of questioning.

"I told you there was not much of interest. Your husband—and it must be assumed my grandfather—was not one for reading novels."

"No, he certainly wasn't. I tried to interest him in poetry once, but to no avail. Roald was investigating the worth of investing in trade with India; that book must be one of the last things he bought before he died." She laid down her fork and gazed at the fire for a moment. "But I have some novels," she added, rousing herself to continue the conversation. "If you would like more entertaining reading material I will lend them to you."

He shrugged and ate some more. He didn't really want to talk about his reading habits; he couldn't explain to himself yet what had interested him in the book on trade, but he had unexpectedly found it fascinating. All his life he had been pushed to find an interest, but his father had nudged him toward politics. He was not interested in politics. He had wanted to join the army, but had been barred from that career.

The idea of trading with the new world or India, however, he found unexpectedly intriguing: boxes shipped from India and arriving at the London docks ready to reveal their fragrant contents of spices and Indian silk, containers from the northern reaches of Canada . . . what they would contain he didn't know, since he had not yet gotten that far in the book.

"You must eat a little more," he said to Nell, and she obediently resumed her meal.

Unreal, he thought, shaking his head as he cut into his own meat and took a bite. It was all so unreal that he should be sitting by the fire in Meadow House, cozily taking a meal with Lady Simmons, whom he had expected to heartily dislike and yet to whom he found himself drawn. He was virtually a prisoner there, and yet except for the lack of exercise, which did bother him—he liked to walk and ride, and both activities had been impossible because of the weather—he had found the retirement and occasional company of Nell and Delphine curiously satisfying.

Even more odd, he had not once been tempted to drink too much, and that was one thing that he had expected to trouble him about being at Meadow

House, given his past experiences and the loathing he held for the house. Mysteriously, much of that feeling had disappeared. Maybe it was only the past inhabitants he had loathed, and not the home. His grandfather and his cousin Roald had been cut from the same cloth. They were both irritable, cold, judgmental, and pompous. Meadow House in the hands of Lady Simmons was warmer, human, altogether happier. It was as if the house pulsed with life, and the heart was Nell. But she would surely take that warmth with her when she left, and Meadow House would revert to its past dullness.

He watched her take her last bite and set her fork aside. She was still frightened and preoccupied, he could tell, about her daughter, even though she had tried to make conversation. He couldn't blame her for that. He barely knew the child and yet he had thought of little else the last few days, but when she would get better . . . *if* she would get better.

He pushed away his plate. "Do you feel that Delphine is recovering? Surely it's good that the rash is gone, and there have been no more breakouts in the house." He had no worry that he was being too abrupt; he was only resuming a conversation that was never truly over between them, in their mutual worry for Delphine's health.

"I'm grateful that no one else has become ill, and that Willie has made such recovery, but Delphine . . . she's not recovered yet."

"Has the doctor been to see her again?" He didn't think the fellow had come back, but wondered about her reaction to mention of the doctor.

"No, Mr. Fitzgerald has not been back; I suspect the weather is too bad to make it up to Meadow

House. In truth, I'm glad. If I had to look at his grim face . . . I would rather doctor her myself and do the best we can, for I don't feel he has ever done any good for her."

"You're wise," Charles said, getting up and moving her small table away from her so she could get the full benefit of the fire's heat. "He seems a nice enough gentleman, but rather rigid and stuck in his ways."

Nell gazed up at him and bit her lip. "I . . . do you know, I have had to counter many of his suggestions, and I have always wondered if I was doing the right thing."

"What do you mean?" Charles asked, straightening.

Braxton came in just then and cleared away the plates. He gave Charles an unfathomable look, and then exited.

Charles poured a glass of sherry for Nell, then repeated his question as he delivered it to her.

"Thank you. I don't usually indulge myself so, but . . ." She sat back in her chair with a sigh and closed her eyes for a moment. But then she roused herself, frowned, and sat up straighter, meeting Charles's questioning gaze. "Dr. Fitzgerald wanted to leech Delphine the last time she was fevered. I couldn't let him do it, she was so pathetically weak! It seemed so much the wrong thing to do, though he said we needed to draw off the bad humors from her blood. He stormed from the house and vowed that I would be the death of her."

"But you weren't."

"No, though he still predicts it every time he sees her. She recovered. And then I added meat to her diet, though everyone has always thought meat so dangerous for children, indigestible. I thought it would help strengthen her, for it does to adult invalids, I know."

Charles grimaced. "How well I remember porridge and gruel from my childhood. It was all we were allowed in the nursery. Our nursemaid was a tyrant. She took over duties from Nanny Lowell— I showed you my poor portrait of that wonderful woman, if you remember—and terrorized both George and myself. No meat, no vegetables, and little of anything but milk, bread, and porridge."

"You were . . . I think you said you were occasionally ill as a child?"

Charles could feel the heat in his face, and it wasn't from the fire. It seemed unmanly to admit so much weakness, especially to someone whom he would have think well of him. But he couldn't change his past. "I was. Sending me away to school was the best thing my father ever did for me; it forced me to fight for my share of the meat. The older form boys would try to bully the smaller boys out of theirs. I became something of a scrapper, despite my . . . despite things." He pushed his lame foot under the chair and tightened his lips into a frown.

She glanced over at him, but didn't question further. "Well, I think that children benefit from the strengthening qualities of meat and vegetables, and variation in their diet. But you would have thought I suggested arsenic the way Doctor Fitzgerald bullied Martha. The poor girl came to me in tears, and I had to have strong words with the doctor. He gloomily predicted that Delphine would be dead by this last August, but instead she gained weight and became quite plump and brown this summer . . . though you w-wouldn't know it now."

Her lip quivered and her lovely eyes teared up, one silvery drop spilling over and trailing down her cheek. She swiped at it surreptitiously and looked away at the fire. Charles moved from his chair to kneel in front of her. He had never seen the kind of devotion she displayed for her daughter; it seemed to him it was a rarity among her class.

"Nell," he said, taking her hand in his own.

She met his gaze, gulping back tears.

"I believe that you know what is best for Delphine," he said, pouring all of his conviction of that truth into his words. "I believe that if you search your heart, you will always do what is best for her. Believe in yourself. Trust yourself." He squeezed her hand.

"How can you say that? What do you know of children?"

"Not a thing," he admitted, "but I *was* a sickly child. I was leeched and cupped and dosed with emetics." As he spoke the words came faster. "I was poked and prodded and the doctors often shook their wise gray heads over me. All their doctoring did was make me more ill. If I had someone to care for me as you do Delphine, I may have recovered more quickly. I'm not saying doctors don't have their place, but sometimes a mother has to do what is best, what she knows in her heart is best. Until doctoring becomes a more exact science, all you can do is trust your instincts."

Her tears dried. She stared into his eyes and he felt a stirring in his heart, almost a pain. So much hope glowed in the blue of her eyes; was he telling her the truth? He believed so.

"But I kept her here, and perhaps if we had moved to London . . ."

"No, Nell." He squeezed her hand again. "Don't do that to yourself. What I said about the fortune teller's message . . . I hope you didn't take that to mean . . ."

She stiffened and pulled her hand away. "Don't be ridiculous. You don't think I've been brooding about that, do you? How absurd!"

Like a chill wind, her expression cooled and he felt the iciness. He had been clumsy, certainly, but he hadn't said anything to incite such a swift change. Lord, but women were difficult to fathom. He moved back and sat down in his chair, but stared at her still, not sure what to say.

Nell was amazed that he appeared to sense her change of mood, even after her blunt words. In her experience men were slow to interpret the feminine temperament. His expression was one of caution, and it would have been diverting if she wasn't so confused by her own feelings.

She didn't need to be coddled by any man, and certainly not by the one sent to drive her out of her home. He knew nothing about her and less about her daughter, so she did not need his reassurance that she was caring for Delphine correctly.

But honestly, it was his mention of the fortune teller that irritated her. She was not superstitious by nature. Why that one long-ago prophecy by a country fair gypsy should haunt her, and why his fresh interpretation of it should worry her, she couldn't explain. Even worse was his intuitive understanding that she was worried by it. No one had ever taken care to delve into her inner feelings, and it felt uncomfortably invasive now, like he knew some secret passage to her heart. She didn't want that, didn't need it. It was too late in her life to find a man who understood her and whose shoulder she could lean on in times of trouble. That was the dream of a green young girl, not a mother and a widow.

He stayed silent, and she regretted her hasty rebuff of his kindness, even if she did question his motivation. His hands were warm, almost as warm as his eyes and open expression. While he knelt in front of her she had felt that warmth.

Roald had been frosty even toward his only child. Whenever Delphine was sick he behaved as though it were Nell's fault. He never ventured up to the nursery to visit her. Charles Blake had been in the nursery more than Roald had in the entirety of Delphine's life.

The fire danced in the grate and a coal popped, an ember rolling toward the carpet. Charles leaned over and pushed it back in with a coal shovel.

"Why do you visit Delphine so often?" she asked, suddenly.

He glanced at her and frowned. "Does she not like it?"

"Of course she does. You are heaven-sent."

"Then why do you ask?"

"I'm curious. You have indicated that you know nothing about children, you have none of your own, and you said that you have never really cared for children. So why Delphine?"

Charles offered a tentative smile. "You are suspicious by nature, aren't you? I suppose I would be too, if I were you. I'm here at my brother's behest, after all, with the message that you must leave Meadow House."

She stayed silent and watched him. He stared into the fire. The house was quiet enough that she could hear the wind rising outside. It was going to be another blizzarding night.

"I guess," he finally said, "that I don't see Delphine as just a child. I mean . . . it's hard to explain. She reached out to me. Why that made a difference I don't know, but it did. She reached out. And once caught, I found . . . I like her. Not as a child, especially . . . oh, that sounds ridiculous." He sighed and frowned, struggling to explain his feelings. "She *is* a child. But she has such a very lively imagination, and is intelligent and charming. Unexpectedly so."

His bewilderment was endearing and she couldn't help but smile. "Especially given her mother's taciturn disposition, is that what you are implying, Sir Charles?"

His eyes lit with merriment and he grinned, his white teeth flashing. "Oh, yes, you are a hard case, Lady Simmons." He stared at her for a long moment. "Nell."

"So is that it? Is it just that I have an overwhelmingly lovely child?"

He shrugged, an habitual gesture with him, she had noticed. He pushed away questions with that shrug, and sometimes pushed away emotions. But this time he spoke, too. "I have found that in some ways children are like dogs."

When she gasped, he held up one hand. "No, shush. Don't get angry. What I mean to say, and am making a mull of, is that children judge you on your behavior toward them, not on any prejudgment that they glean from adult opinions."

"Child personality traits aside, Delphine could have no such set of prejudices about you. She didn't know you existed until you came into her room."

Charles gave her a quick sideways look. "Do you mean to say that you never spoke of me in front of her . . . even when you thought she was sleeping?"

She felt herself flushing to the roots of her hair. How appalling, to be caught in such a way. "Why do you say that?"

"Things Delphine has said in our private conversations. I don't think," he said, dryly, "that she would know otherwise to ask me if I truly was a wastrel and a rake, though she didn't, she explained charmingly, know what such things were."

She bit her lip, but then saw his mouth split into an engaging grin.

"So, is it you or your dour maid, Lundy, who has been saying such villainous things about me near that poor child?"

"Charles, I'm sorry," she said, feeling perilously close to tears or laughter, and not knowing which was appropriate.

"It's all right," he said. "Because I was able to assure her that though I may have been somewhat of a wastrel in my life, in my own estimation I am not, nor have I ever been, a rake. I'm not nearly accomplished enough at villainy for that."

"Oh, Charles!" Nell gave up then and laughed, really *laughed* for the first time in a very long time.

TWELVE

"Why do you never start the story with what happened, what you did that the king rewarded you by making you a knight?"

Charles, seated easily on the edge of Delphine's bed, gazed down at her pinched face, wan and pale in the flickering light of the candle, and tried to come up with an answer that would leave that part of the story untold.

He glanced over at the cot in the corner. Nell was there, curled up and dozing, a shawl over her. Just the night before they had sat by the fire in the library and talked, and he had seen sides of her he still didn't truly understand. He hadn't seen her all day, and now afternoon was stretching into early evening, the pale winter sunlight slanting into the room through the frosted windowpanes. Nell looked childlike herself, curled up with her face cradled on her clasped hands.

His attention was pulled back to Delphine by her tugging at his sleeve.

"Why?" she asked, her bright gaze fixed on his face.

He smiled. "Why. Why, why, why! You ask that often." It was such a child question.

"Because I want to know the answer. Why do you not just tell me, and then I won't have to ask why again?"

He chuckled at her reasoning. "Perhaps not to that particular query, but I'm sure you'll find another." He remembered following the gardener around at his father's estate and asking him "why" about everything, from why plants grew to why rain came from clouds. He gazed into the blue of her innocent eyes and wished he had a better answer as to the event behind his knighting and why he didn't speak of it, but he didn't. If it was just that he was humble! If only it could be because he truly didn't want to speak of such a noble deed, but alas! Such was not the truth of the matter.

"So, why?"

"It's a private matter, lass. Just between me and the Prince Regent."

"Is it a secret?"

He hesitated. "Not exactly. It's just private. Do you understand?"

"I suppose." She wriggled under the covers. "Is the prince your friend?"

"He was. But I'm afraid he is a very expensive friend to have, and I haven't any money."

Sleepily she yawned and stretched. "I do," she murmured. "I'm very rich."

"Are you?"

"Yes. I have a box with some pennies in it, and if we go to London I shall buy a yellow dress and a lemon ice and go to see the lions in the Tower."

"I would be honored to take you to see them, if you would allow me. I think you would look better in pink than yellow, though."

"But yellow is my favorite color, like sunshine."

"But pink would suit your blond hair and pink cheeks." He tweaked one.

She appeared to consider his suggestion. "A pink dress, then. But with blue bows?"

"Certainly with blue bows. And shoes of Morocco leather."

"I'd like that." She yawned. "And then will you tell me why you were knighted?"

"Perhaps. You should sleep now, little cousin of mine." He pulled the blankets up to her chin.

"Am I getting better? I don't like being sick all the time," she fretted.

Charles leaned over and felt her forehead. It felt cooler than it had the day before, and she was not damp. She had certainly been livelier today, and had stayed awake longer. He felt a tickle of hope in the pit of his stomach. He straightened and gazed down at her. "Do you *feel* better?"

She nodded.

"Then yes, I think you are getting better."

She stretched and yawned again, fighting sleep, it seemed to Charles.

"Can I take you outside tomorrow to show you the knight in the garden?" she murmured. "It doesn't look much like your painting, you know. You were not very good at drawing."

He chuckled at her honesty. "No," he said gently, but firmly. "You will not be that much better for some time. We must take care of you, and you must do exactly what your mother tells you to."

"But I wish I could show you the statue! It glitters in the light, just like the armor on the knight in the story, goldy-colored, though I know it's not real gold. It's just ice. But I want to see it again."

"Miss Delphine Blake," he said, with an attempt at severity that he felt ill suited him. "You must behave and do what you are told if you truly want to get better."

"I will."

"See that you do, even if the medicine tastes foul, as it so often does." Charles made a strangled face and Delphine laughed out loud.

Nell stirred on the cot and looked at them both sleepily. "What is the joke?"

"Nothing," Charles said. "I just made a face, and Miss Delphine chose to think it was humorous." He dropped a wink at the child and she giggled, hiding her face under the covers. He turned his attention to the mother. "I'm sorry we woke you up, Nell."

She sat and moved to the edge of the cot, rubbing her eyes. She pushed her gray gown down over her legs and put her feet on the floor. "No, Charles, I'm sorry I was sleeping. It was rude of me."

"Don't be absurd," he said lightly. He turned back to Delphine. "And now I must go back downstairs," he said, "to the dungeon." He pulled a sad face and the child smiled up at him. But she was finally surrendering to sleep, and Charles hoped he had not overstayed his visit, for her own good. He tucked her in, put his painting of the statue at the end of her bed propped up by a pillow, as she always insisted he do, and gave a little wave to Nell. To his surprise she rose and followed him out to the hall, still rubbing the sleep from her eyes.

She closed the door behind her and said, "I really need a breath of fresh air, Charles. I haven't been outside for days." She rubbed her arms at the chill air of the hallway. "Would you walk outside with me? I know it's cold, but . . ."

"Not too cold for a short walk. I'd like it if you would show me the statue of the knight, so I can tell Delphine that I have seen it. I remember that it's in the knot garden, but with the heavy snow I can't tell which side of the house that's on. It's odd, but I just don't remember."

"That's a wonderful idea. Let me make sure Martha can watch Delphine for me—I think she's up having tea with Willie—and I'll meet you in the hall."

Charles made his way downstairs slowly, intrigued by Nell's change of demeanor. He went to his suite for his greatcoat and muffler; though Godfrey was not to be found he managed to retrieve the required items from his wardrobe and descended to the first floor. Once Nell joined him, they left the house through a back door, a swifter route to the garden that he remembered from his childhood.

She shivered. "I should have suggested this earlier. It's getting dark."

"There's still some light, and the sunset is going to peek through those trees on the distant rise any moment."

"Follow me," she said, and took his arm.

The ground was icy, but the gardener had shoveled a path through the garden, likely for his own convenience. In the fading light the sky was changing from dove gray to a bruised plum, and Charles said, "I was here for Christmas a couple of times when Grandfather was alive. I had been sick for a long time one year, but when we were sent here, I spent all my time outside just to avoid him. He was a Tartar."

"Your father was Roald's father's brother, is that right?"

"Yes, you have it exactly, his youngest brother; about nine years separated them. My father was not able to marry until he was almost thirty . . . a younger son, you know, while Roald's father married young. That accounts for the age difference between George and me, and Roald. There were a couple of brothers between them, but no one ever spoke of them much. I don't suppose Roald ever did. One, Benjamin, the second oldest, had a daughter named India who died as an infant, and then he died himself soon after—very tragic, I understand—and then there was our cousins Lester and Latimer's father; Marden Blake came to a bad end, so I was told. So did Lester and Latimer, though I don't suppose dying in a swimming accident or in the army can be truly counted as a bad end. Just unlucky."

"Not a fortunate family."

"Hmm. No, not fortunate in many ways, but these things do happen." He didn't bother telling her about George's preoccupation with the supposed Simmons Curse, for it was such errant nonsense and it made not a particle of sense, though it did explain his brother's carefulness with his health. A string of unfortunate deaths had been strung into some kind of deadly hex by his brother's superstitious mind, even though no one in any other generation had seen it thus.

They went on, with the frost nipping at their extremities, until they rounded the house to the statuary garden. Just then a ray of sun broke through the trees and purple sunset clouds, and fortunately made its way to the knight.

It glowed, a thick layer of ice transforming it from greened bronze to purest gold.

"This is what Delphine was speaking of, her gilded knight," Nell said, breathless from their energetic walk. "Somehow it has become the knight in her fairy tale."

Charles pulled off his glove and reached out, touching the gilt surface. "Just an illusion, though, his gilding. It is merely frost and ice."

"Children have trouble distinguishing the difference between an illusion and the truth."

He cast her a swift glance. Such a cynical, sad little speech. Where had she learned such philosophy? The ice melted under the warmth of his hand, and he pulled back, wiping his wet hand on his greatcoat, shoving his fingers back into his glove to warm them up. "Or maybe it's just that to an innocent mind there isn't a lot of difference between what looks gold and what is. Delphine knows the truth, that it's just a coating of ice. But her imagination is wiser, maybe, and tells her it's gold."

The sun lowered some more and the statue became drab again, just dross coated in ice.

As they walked on, driven by some mutual but unspoken agreement, they came to the edge of the terraced garden. They stopped and gazed out across the sloping grass yard, now covered in drifts and mounds of snow, humped in great heaps over shrubs and small trees.

"I have never seen this much snow in all the years I have been mistress of Meadow House."

"George and I were here last in . . ." Charles stopped. "Good Lord," he said, "do you realize I can't even name the season? I truly spent that awful time in a complete fog of alcohol."

"It was spring, I remember. You drank so much Mrs. Howard would not let the maids rouse you in the morning, and instead did it herself. She said she daily expected you to expire, and did not want one of her maids to find you in bed dead . . . or worse."

"Worse? I wonder what the worse was?"

"Dead and nude, I think."

"Scandalous," Charles said and chuckled. "And I thought I was a particular favorite of hers!"

Nell laughed with him, a silvery sound in the gray twilight, and Charles felt his heart thud. Why did her simplest gestures affect him so?

"You are now," she said, clutching his arm and squeezing it. "Somehow you have won over my staff, and they were prepared to despise you, you know."

Combating the sick thumping of his heart, Charles worked to make his tone casual. "Well, as brother of the new Lord Simmons it's perhaps just that it is in their best interest to befriend me."

Nell pulled her arm from his. "How cynical, Charles."

"Don't pull away from me, Nell. I'm sorry if that sounded cynical."

She stopped and stared up at him, the fading light making her oval face a pale disk. "No, don't apologize. We each have our cynical moments, don't we?" She tilted her head to one side. "I don't understand you at all, you know. You're not at all what I remember, nor what I expected. I should dislike you, I should rebuff you, but . . ."

"But what?"

"I find I can't," she finished simply. "You do the most unexpected things, like apologize to me when you think you have offended me."

"Is that so strange?"

"It is in my experience, for a man anyway. My husband little regarded my feelings on matters and wouldn't have noticed if I was offended. And that was what I expected from marriage, since it was how my father treated my mother and both of his daughters."

"Not all men are the same," he said, gently.

She gazed at him steadily, her head still tilted to one side. "I'm beginning to understand that."

"Nell . . ." He stopped, not sure what he wanted to say.

She drifted closer to him and gazed up into his eyes. "Yes?"

He could smell her, she was so close, the scent of lavender lingering in her hair and clothes. Even bundled in a coat and with a scarf around her cloud of blond hair she was lovely, enticingly female, more truly a woman than any lady he had ever met. Her pink lips hovered temptingly beneath his, and he was being drawn in, suffocated by a need that squeezed his heart and constricted his breathing.

But to what end? She would never be anything more to him than a friend and relation. He had nothing to offer, nothing that she could ever need. He could delude himself that he might come to mean something to her, but it would be a lie.

As if she sensed his uncertainty, she drifted back, turned away, and strolled down the path. "Let's talk of something else," she said, "other than . . . than whatever we were speaking of."

He swallowed. "Certainly," he said, struggling to make his tone natural and unaffected. "You begin, my lady Nell."

"All right," she said. She walked farther along the path, avoiding his eyes. "I haven't been to London in many years, not since my sister and I had our come-outs. Have I mentioned my sister, Elizabeth? I don't suppose I have. She . . . she married that same year and moved to Italy soon after. And then . . . and then I married Roald."

She paused and looked back at him, but then turned away again and began chattering. "So, has London changed at all in the last ten or twelve years? Or is the Season still as I remember, a mad whirl of balls and fetes? And is Vauxhall still as magical as it seemed when I was seventeen?"

THIRTEEN

The awkward moment passed. He had kissed her so naturally before; what was different this time? He couldn't say, but something in his heart had shifted. Kissing her now would break him; he didn't love her—*couldn't* love her—but he was perilously close, and it was uncharted waters for him. Kissing her one more time might have sent him into that dangerous territory. If he had thought there was a chance they would ever be able to have more than friendship, he would have dismissed caution, but there were far too many obstacles between them.

They talked and walked and he told her what he knew of current society. It had been many years since the year of her come-out, and she had never even danced the waltz. She talked about her sister, and her late brother, and how much she missed them both. When the darkening sky meant it was too cold to stand the outdoors anymore, they went inside and had dinner together in the morning parlor, then sat for a while in the library before she retreated to her daughter's room.

Charles said good night to her in the library, telling her he intended to read for a while before retiring to his own room. It was a lie; he was exhausted and couldn't wait to go to bed, but he couldn't bear for her to see how laborious his climb up the long curved staircase was going to be. After so much walking and being up and down the steep stairs to Delphine's room, his foot was tight in his boot and the ascension was going to take a while. Every step felt like he was dragging his foot behind him, and as he limped into his bedroom suite, Godfrey looked up from a book he was reading.

"Sir Charles! Are you hurt?" He leaped up and threw the book down on the chair.

"No . . . I hurt, but I'm not hurt, if you can make any sense of that. It's my damned foot; it's throbbing like the devil is needling me with his pitchfork. Help me take my boot off." He collapsed on the edge of the bed and Godfrey knelt in front of him and tugged at the boot. "Ow," Charles yelped. "Damn, it hasn't hurt like that since I was a lad."

"You've overdone it, sir." Godfrey more gently worked the boot off, and then removed the other one.

Charles brought his foot up, pulled his stocking off and glared at his damnable foot, clumsy and swollen now. It was twisted as if he had been in an accident, but it was just the way he was born. Godfrey put his boots away and then came back. When Charles looked up at him it was to see an expression of sympathy on his face.

"Don't say a word," Charles warned.

There passed between them an unspoken understanding. It was said that no man was a hero to his valet, and Charles could well see why. Who saw a man's frailties more clearly? Godfrey's silence was valuable. One thing Charles could never bear was pity.

"Why don't I get a basin of water, sir, and you can soak your foot."

Charles nodded. He stared down at his feet, the one so perfectly formed and the other twisted and clumsy. The only other people to have seen his feet naked in the recent past were Godfrey and his bootmaker. It had been a long while since he had been with a woman, and yet it wasn't his lameness that held him back. The kind of girls he frequented didn't care about that kind of thing, and if they made fun of him behind his back, he never knew of it.

He just hadn't been interested for some time. Forgetfulness and escape had been bought with other vices; drinking and gambling whiled away hours of dreary time.

But if one was to be with a lady . . . a wife. She would have to see it, know he was imperfect, be reminded of his lameness every time they lay down together. It was not as if it was a secret, for he did limp when he was tired. But booted it looked relatively normal; that one malformed limb . . . he held his foot out in front of him. It bothered him more than he had ever admitted.

Godfrey came back with an enamel basin of water and salts and Charles lowered his foot into it. He supposed there were some women in the world who would not think less of a man for such a thing. Someone like . . . Nell, perhaps. He pushed the heels of his hands into his forehead. He had to stop thinking of her like that . . . he *had* to. There was no future, no hope, no possibility.

"You mustn't overdo it again, sir," Godfrey said, his tone anxious.

"No, I suppose not," Charles replied, letting his hands drop to his lap. "But all we did was to walk outside. I have walked as long before in London without this consequence."

"Walking out in this weather is more difficult. The ground is icy, and one holds oneself differently; you likely put more strain on your foot."

"P'raps." The warm water was helping ease the ache, and he sighed, swishing his foot in the warmth. "Nell wanted to walk. We talked about London. Maybe I'll be able to see her and Delphine when they are there." There was silence for a moment, and he looked up to find Godfrey arrested in the act of folding a towel.

"You won't be able to see anyone if you have nowhere to live," the valet said. "And you will have nowhere to live if your brother doesn't feel you have come through with your end of the deal."

"You don't need to remind me of that," Charles said, unpleasantly brought back to reality.

"Perhaps I do."

"You are being unspeakably impertinent," Charles said. Godfrey put down a folded towel on the floor by the basin. "Anyway, we can do nothing with the weather like this. There hasn't even been any mail for a week or more."

The valet straightened and said casually, "The gardener, I have heard, believes that we will have a break in this snow and iciness soon, though." He sighed and turned away to the dressing table, absently straightening a line of brushes and combs.

"Sir, for your own good you must press Lady Simmons to move to London."

"Enough!" Charles said, glaring at his valet, who turned to meet his gaze. "Her child is ill. If you feel I'm going about things in the wrong way, then you are free to leave my service this minute, but I will *not* be bullied by my valet, even if every last man in London is. At least most are wise enough to confine their bullying to issues of dress and hairstyle. It is my life, if I need to remind you."

They stared at each other for a minute, and finally Godfrey, with an unfathomable expression, said, "You care for Lady Simmons very much, don't you?"

"I do." Charles looked down at the floor and contemplated that simple affirmation. "I do. I wish I could allow myself to feel more, but I do like her very much. For the first time in my life I feel like I am of some use to someone, rather than being a damned nuisance. I came here thinking she was an icicle, only to find . . . Godfrey, I've never met anyone like her. She has lived only to put others' good above her own, and she deserves to have someone look after her in the same way. She deserves a man . . . a *husband*, who will put her good before his own and think of her for once. Roald didn't do so."

"In my experience, gentlemen expect that things will be much the opposite in marriage, that a lady will put his good before her own."

Charles nodded agreement. "I suppose that is often the case. She's so grateful for every little courtesy, and so surprised by them. My mother said those attentions are every lady's due, and that a woman should be protected and cherished, but it appears that few men were raised as I was." He put his foot on the towel and wiped it dry. It felt a little better, but still ached. "Certainly not my father. I doubt he ever thought of Mother unless she was before him."

"I don't believe I've ever heard you speak of your mother, sir."

"No, I seldom talk of her. But I think of her often. Very often."

Silently, Godfrey took the basin away, and then helped his employer undress for bed. It was only nine-thirty, but Charles was tired.

As the valet attended to the night candle and prepared to exit, he stopped once and turned to Charles, his expression unreadable. "Sir, if you asked me, I would tell you that the staff is very much of your opinion, that Lady Simmons deserves to find someone who will look after her and Miss Delphine better than the late Lord Simmons did." He paused, then added, "But not once have I heard them say that she needs to find a wealthy husband."

Charles sat up in bed and exclaimed, "What the devil do you mean by that?"

"Nothing at all, sir." Godfrey moved serenely toward the dressing room, where he had his own bed. "It was just an observation."

When Nell entered her daughter's room it was to find Martha folding some clean linens and Lundy tidying Delphine's bedside table. The small room seemed crowded with people after she entered. Delphine sat up in her bed and was watching, still

pale but with more animation than Nell had yet
seen.

She leaned over and kissed her daughter's forehead, and exclaimed, "So cool! Your forehead is
quite cool, my dearest!"

"Yes, and she has been plaguing us with questions
this half hour," Lundy said, squeezing past Martha.
"About when she may get up and go outside."

"Not for a while, dear." Nell sat on the edge of the
bed. "You have been very ill. We won't risk your
health now that it appears you are getting better."
She closed her eyes, said a silent prayer of thanks,
and opened them again to find her daughter's inquisitive gaze on her face. "Charles and I went for a
walk," she said, brightly, not wanting Delphine to
sense anything amiss, "because he wanted to see the
statue himself and let you know he had seen it."

"Is it still covered in ice?" Delphine asked, bounc-
ing once on the bed. "Oh, I do wish I could see it."

Nell put her hands on her daughter's thin shoulders. "I wish you could too, darling, but for now you
must make do with the painting." She retrieved it off
the floor where it had fallen and propped it up again
at the end of the bed. "Do you still want it there?"

"Yes! It makes me think of outside, and the
statue . . . though . . ." Delphine gave her mother
a shame-faced look. "It's not very good, is it?"

"No," Nell laughed. "It's not, but you can tell
what it is, and Charles wasn't much older than you
when he painted it. So for his age at the time I
think it is very good." She gazed at the painting and
smiled, noting details she hadn't seen before. The
young Charles Blake had put in an odd rendering

of some animal at the base of the statue, a rabbit or a dog, or maybe a cat, it was impossible to tell.

Delphine settled down some, and Nell pulled the covers up over her thin legs and frame. "You know, it's late; you should be sleeping."

"I *was* sleeping. I feel that I've been sleeping for days. I don't want to sleep anymore." She punctuated that assertion with a yawn, but sat up again, the blankets falling away from her. "Mama, why is Charles here? He says he's my cousin. Is that so?"

"Yes, it's true. Your papa and he were cousins, so that makes you his cousin, too. He just came for a visit." *And to drive us from our home,* Nell added to herself. Though, far from pressing, he had become more like a pleasant houseguest, a friend to the family. And something more to herself, though she refused to reflect on how close she came to kissing him as they strolled outside. She had wanted to, had practically invited him to kiss her, but he had, for some unfathomable reason, withdrawn. Unfathomable, she thought, because she could see in his eyes that he had wanted to take her in his arms.

Delphine fidgeted, picking up her doll and squeezing it to her. As she cradled it, Nell felt her breath catch in her chest and tears well in her eyes. It seemed so long since her daughter acted so; during this illness Delphine's complete lack of interest in her doll, who was her best friend and had heard every whispered confidence of her childhood, had been alarming. It truly seemed that she was recovering, at last.

"Can Charles stay here with us always?" Delphine asked, wistfully.

"No, he can't."

"Why not, if he is family?"

What could she say, that he was Delphine's family, but not *her* family? "Not all family lives together, Delphine. We know very little about him, really. And he has a place to live in London. Now, chatterbox, you must lie down and at least pretend that you are going to go to sleep."

She obeyed, but kept talking. "And we are going to London, too, aren't we, mama? Charles said he'll take me to see the lions in London when we go. I am to wear a pink dress with blue bows and we'll eat lemon ices."

Nell sighed in exasperation and caught Lundy's snort, of disbelief or humor, she couldn't tell which.

Martha stood nearby openly listening to the conversation as she hugged a stack of linens to her chest. "My lady," she said.

"Yes, Martha?"

"May Willie . . . I mean, would Willie stay here and work, or come to London with us?"

"I don't know!" She pulled up Delphine's covers with an irritated tug, but felt a pang of remorse when she saw Martha's ashen face and crestfallen expression. "I haven't made any decisions yet. Lord, why is everyone pushing me to go to London?"

"Everyone?" Lundy tipped her head to one side. "Who is pushing you to go to London?"

Nell refused to answer. "Martha, don't worry about anything else. You may go and tuck Willie in if you like, and then go to your own room. I'll take care of Delphine tonight. I think your brother will be well enough to resume his duties in a couple of days, but for now I want him to be cautious. Mrs.

Howard has said that one feature of scarlatina is the possibility of rebounding if one is not careful."

"Yes, ma'am."

"And Martha," Nell said, as the maid moved to the door with slumped shoulders. "We can speak of Willie's coming with us to London tomorrow, if you like."

"Yes, my lady," Martha said. With a pretty curtsy and flashing smile she flounced out the door.

"She is far too pretty for London," Lundy said, darkly.

"Why?" Delphine asked, glancing from her mother to the maid and back again.

Nell gave Lundy a warning look, and turned back to her daughter. "She just meant that Martha is so pretty she would outshine every other girl there."

"I think so too," Delphine said, snuggling down in her bed, drawing her doll to her thin frame and wrapping her arms around her. "She would like Willie to come, I think. Do you know, Mama, I think Martha likes Mr. Godfrey . . . he is Charles's manservant, you know," she added, with a wise little nod.

"Why do you say that?" Nell said, taken aback by such a pronouncement.

Delphine's narrow face pinched in a meditative expression. "Martha told me that she has never met anyone like Mr. Godfrey. She says that he is so much a gentleman, one would never take him for a servant. And she said that he is so polite, and bows to her when he sees her, and always asks after her brother, and about herself. And he told her to be careful, for it would be a shame if she came down with the same disease as Willie and me."

Nell exchanged a doubtful look with Lundy. Was

there something to worry about? Was Martha's head being turned? Lundy shook her head as if in answer, but Nell knew it would never do to talk about it in front of her daughter. She had learned that even when she appeared asleep, Delphine sometimes caught on to things that were said. Mrs. Howard would know if anything was going on.

"Well, that rather says that Mr. Godfrey is very kind, doesn't it?"

"Yes, but Martha has never spoken about any other men servants, not even Braxton, who all the maids think is so handsome, even Adele."

"Enough about that, Delphine," Nell said firmly. "We don't gossip about anyone, servants or not. You must go back to sleep." She felt her forehead, and added, "You're becoming a little fevered, and we don't want you to become ill again. You're so much better today, but you mustn't overdo it; you won't be able to get out of bed if you become sick again."

When Delphine appeared to be drifting off to sleep, Nell stood and watched her for a while, joined soon by Lundy.

"What a lot of things a child thinks and sees and hears that we don't know," the maid observed.

Nell put one finger to her mouth in warning. "I know," she whispered. "More than I ever expected."

"Especially about Sir Charles." Lundy gazed up at Nell. "She has taken to the gentleman."

"She'll forget about him when Sir Charles becomes bored and goes back to his drinking and gambling." Her words surprised even herself. Was it what she truly thought, or was she trying to insulate herself from his unexpected charm?

For he had insinuated himself into her heart. She

cared about him. Against reason, against all sense, she found him charming, good-natured, excellent company, and . . . and his care for her, his concern for her comfort was unplanned and unrehearsed. It was not, despite what her cynical self would say, a ploy to disarm her.

But beyond how he made her feel—she had forgotten what it felt like to have a man treat her so gently and with such great care, as if she were a fragile flower to be cherished and cared for—his own vulnerability seared her to the soul. What had touched her most all evening was that she could tell how fiercely he was concentrating to keep from limping as they said good night. She had caught an expression of pain on his face, and it had made her wonder how much his foot hurt him. Her emotional response to that endearing streak of male pride and fear of appearing weak had surprised her . . . and frightened her.

She could care for him. She could even love him if she allowed herself, and that admission was astonishing, given her determination never to marry again, nor to even think of anything beyond raising her daughter.

She could love him, but inevitably, he would complicate her life if she continued to allow him such admittance to her heart. Her daughter was already half in love with him; would she follow?

No, the cost was too high. What did she really know of him, beyond his unexpected charm and his kindness to her? Was he only softening her so she would be more amenable to coaxing? There were too many risks attached to letting her wayward heart grow attached, and she would need to be stern with herself. There was no sense in bringing heartache into her life.

She had already decided to leave as soon as she judged Delphine well enough to travel, but she and Charles had not spoken of it. If she told him, then he might leave her alone. In her present vulnerable state, that was an outcome to be hoped for. Sighing heavily, she turned away from the bed.

"Will you be sleeping in your own room tonight, my lady?" Lundy asked, bundling her knitting into a bag.

"No. I'll sleep on the cot, as usual."

"You really don't need to," the maid said, reproof in her voice. "Not with Martha just in the next room. She would respond instantly if Delphine were to take ill again. Or she could even sleep in here on the cot, if you're worried about a relapse."

"Lundy, I've made my decision. If Delphine is still better in the morning, then I'll think about it."

FOURTEEN

Three more days passed. Charles visited Delphine every morning and every afternoon, and even managed a little time with Nell, though for some unfathomable reason their conversation was often strained and unnatural. He knew his own dilemma; he wanted to kiss her again, but knew he shouldn't. He cared for her more deeply with every passing day but knew it could come to nothing. All he could do was avoid thinking about his own feelings and concentrate on Delphine, and her marvelous returning health.

He had been at Meadow House for three weeks, and in all that time he realized he had no idea what was happening in the wide world beyond the estate. It was a peaceful existence, but couldn't last.

The morning parlor, where he habitually ate breakfast, lingering over coffee sometimes, hoping to be joined by Nell, was flooded with sunlight. Icicles that had decorated the window overhangs were dripping and glittering in the morning sun. The gilded knight in the garden would likely be melting too, and returning to its dreary appearance of tarnished bronze.

He ate his breakfast slowly, deliberately emptying

his mind of all thought. Too many unexpected plans popped into his mind when he least expected it. When they got to London, he would think, he would take Nell and Delphine to see the Serpentine in Hyde Park. Delphine would enjoy sailing a toy boat there, perhaps.

And then reason would intrude; Nell had given him no indication that they would continue to see each other when they moved to London. She couldn't avoid him at Meadow House, but once installed at Dorsey House in Chelsea, she would resume her life, reacquaint herself with old friends . . . there would be no place for him there.

That was the circular nature of his thoughts, and it was dizzying. He could not restrain himself from wanting things he would never attain and planning things he could never do.

Braxton came in and laid a stack of letters beside his plate. "The gardener made it down to the village finally, sir, now that everything is melting, and this mail was waiting for you."

Charles gazed at the stack and pushed his half-full plate away. The top one was addressed in George's slanting hand. And the next one down, too, and the one after that. They were all from George.

Well, there was no point in reading the earliest ones. He pulled out the bottom one and opened it.

Couched in hysterical terms, it claimed that Charles was dodging his familial responsibilities, and that George was going to have no choice but to tell the duns—who were already plaguing him as to his brother's whereabouts, as was a large-fisted gentleman who said he was Charles's landlady's son—where he was and how to find him.

Not only would he do that, George said, but he would find a way to tie up Charles's allowance for the next quarter, too, leaving him in an even worse state.

Charles had better think of how he intended to live for the next few years, because it would take very stringent measures to get out of the kind of debt he was in if his allowance was stopped or delayed, George said. Charles would have nowhere to live, and nothing to live on, and he could expect no help from his family. If he did not do his duty, and very swiftly too, and get Lady Simmons and her febrile infant out of Meadow House, he would be destitute.

Laying the letter down with a sigh, Charles stared out the window. Meltwater trickled down the pane, and he limped over to look out. Sun shone and the snowdrifts had shrunk just in the hour or so the sun had been out. The landscape stretched out to the horizon, with a few dots of green indicating that in some places even the grass was showing where the drifted snow was thinnest.

The reckoning had arrived, it seemed, and the reminder of his purpose in being there was timely. He had no idea what Nell intended to do. In fact he had been blithely content to let fate take care of itself, enjoying the family feel of Nell and Delphine's company and his new appreciation for Meadow House.

But it was time that the lady answered some questions. Delphine was recovering apace, and yet no preparations were being made to move. Surely if Nell ever intended to leave, things would need to be done, the estate would need to be assessed, and an exact statement of what belonged to Meadow House and what Nell could take with her to Dorsey

House should be made. The lawyer who drew up the late Lord Simmons's will would need to be contacted.

But everything just continued in the same calm manner, day by day, week by week, as if she never intended to leave. It couldn't continue. Nell needed to be reminded, perhaps, that it was her duty to pass on the Simmons legacy to the new Lord Simmons.

Charles stumped out of the room to the library. He needed to think and decide how he was going to go about the delicate chore, made more difficult by how much he liked Delphine, and how deeply he had come to care for Nell.

If circumstances were different, if he was different—

But he wasn't. He was Sir Charles Blake, impoverished younger son, destitute and relying on his brother for help to get out of his latest muddle. And if George was going to help him, then he had to have what he wanted . . . no, what was *owed* to him. It was only his due George was looking for, after all, not any extraordinary boon.

The necessary conversation with Nell was not something Charles looked forward to, but it had to be done. It was only just, the law, Nell's obligation. And he would have to keep telling himself that, over and over again, when he gazed into her lovely blue eyes and sweet expression.

Nell, about to reenter her daughter's room, paused just beyond the door and watched Martha encouraging Delphine to sit on the edge of the bed and take her breakfast at a little table drawn up to her.

"Now, Miss Delphine, you don't want to stay in that bed too much longer, do you? Willie asked after you, you know. He says he's ever so sorry if he gave you that dreadful scarlatina."

"It's not his fault, Martha. Perhaps I gave it to him."

"Oh, no, I don't think so. He was back at our ma and pa's house the Sunday before, you know, and it seems he might have caught it there. Terrible thing."

"But I'm getting better now, Martha, you said so yourself." Delphine sighed and played with her spoon. "I wish Mama would not worry so. I know she watches me at night. What if she makes herself sick with worry? I *have* to get up and walk."

"Not yet, miss, not yet." Martha, sitting on the low stool by the bedside, put out one hand and caressed Delphine's thin shoulder. "Not yet. Tomorrow, if you're a good girl today. But only a step or two, mind, and no acrobatics. No climbing of trees or swinging from bellpulls."

Delphine giggled and ate some of her porridge, but then pushed it away. Nell entered the room with a new understanding.

"I think, my love," she said to Delphine, her tone deliberately cheerful and unconcerned, "that I will be moving back into my own room today. You're *so* much better, and Martha can stay in here for a night or two, until we're sure you're all right on your own."

Martha rose, smiled, and said, "Yes, my lady. I'd be happy to stay in here for a couple of nights. I'll take this downstairs," she finished, taking the tray and heading for the door.

"You must really believe I'm getting better!" Delphine exclaimed to her mother, moving back under the covers.

Nell propped her pillow up against the head of the bed and sat down with her daughter. "I do. You know, I think I have been staying in here because I like being close to you, not really because I was worried. You are so much better. And I heard you and Martha talking about walking. She's exactly right. A few steps tomorrow, and a little more each day."

"And then outside?"

Nell sighed and shook her head. "Slowly, Delphine, slowly. You've been in bed for several weeks, and you cannot expect to be running and jumping in a day or two. You will need to be a little patient while you recover your strength. Now, shall we play a card game for a while?"

When her daughter began to yawn, Nell retreated, letting Martha stay with her. She couldn't inflict her own fears on Delphine. It wasn't fair and it wasn't wise. She had always known Delphine was intelligent and sensitive, aware of much more than the adults around her sometimes thought, but it was startling to hear what hypotheses she fabricated from those behaviors. It was human nature, maybe, to assume the worst, and children, it seemed, were not immune from those dangerous assumptions.

She made her way down the stairs to the second floor and toward her own room as she considered how easy it would be to cripple Delphine with love, so afraid her daughter would fall ill again that she wouldn't let her even get out of bed. She had been perilously close to doing just that. By devoting herself so fiercely to her daughter, she could actually hurt her, it seemed, as impossible as that sounded. When they moved to London she would have to be sure she found interests of her own, things to look forward to beyond Delphine and her health. Any excess, even of devotion, was a harmful thing, it seemed.

Her room, for three weeks used only as a dressing chamber, was dim and cold, and she strode across to the window and threw open the curtains. It was raining. It was raining and she hadn't even been aware of it!

February was one day away, the long month of January finally coming to an end. Spring was on its way, and perhaps it was finally time to set a tentative date for their move to London, and whatever awaited them there.

She stared out the window and rubbed her arms, trying to warm herself up.

It was not as if she wasn't ready. Most of her own things were already packed and stored at Dorsey House in London, though she had never bothered to tell the new Lord Simmons that. The bank in London had her jewels. They had been sent by messenger soon after Roald had died, as in mourning one didn't need jewels. And other than that there were just her clothes and a few other personal items that would need to go.

But she was afraid, so afraid. Afraid of life, afraid of . . . everything. Things were so simple when there was just Delphine to care for. Life in London meant complications, people, social calls to make. Lately she had retreated from almost everything that made her feel vulnerable, even Charles.

Even this room. She stood in the center and turned, slowly, in a circle. She had hated it from the day she had come as a young bride, but intimidated by Roald she had never changed it, and then when

Delphine was born and they were both sick for so long, it just didn't seem important. But she hated it. She hated the grim paintings of ancestors who frowned disapprovingly down at her as she tossed and turned in her lonely huge bed. She hated the bed draperies, their deep blood red a hideous reminder of fever and contagion. And hemorrhaging. She had lost a son before Delphine was born, and though she put it from her mind most of the time, occasionally it came back to haunt her with memories of blood and pain and illness.

She utterly despised the heavy Jacobean furniture, the distance from the stairs to Delphine's room, and the view from the window of the road. She hated everything about it.

So why should she stay in it when just down the hall was the Ivory Room, her ideal, with lovely French furnishings painted in white and gold, and brocade drapes the color of cream. The view was of the garden, and it was next to the stairs to Delphine's room.

She swiftly made up her mind. For however long she had to stay in this house, she would not sleep in this mausoleum of Simmons ancestors. She exited the room and called from the top of the stairs. "Braxton! Braxton!"

The footman came running, a look of worry on his handsome face. "My lady?"

"Don't worry," she said, "Nothing is wrong. But I need John and Andrew and that strong young lad they just hired for the garden . . . what is his name?"

"Jem, my lady."

"Yes, Jem. Call them in and tell them I wish some things moved. I'm changing rooms."

Lundy dashed into the downstairs hall and looked up, dabbing milk from her lips. "My lady? What's wrong?"

"Nothing. Come up when you are done your lunch. But eat first. Come to the Ivory Room. I'll have some things for you to do." She whirled and went back to her new room. Changing her life would not wait until she got to London. It would start now, here.

Charles, irritable from a midday nap he had not intended to take, was awoken by a rumbling sound. Was it thunder . . . a storm? He threw off the light blanket he had over him and dashed to the window, but there was just a steady drizzle coming down, no sign of thunder. He limped over to the door. A maid ran by his room and he grabbed her arm. "What's going on?"

"Her ladyship . . . she's moving, sir."

"Moving?"

Charles dug the sleep from his eyes and, heart thumping, marched down the hall until he came to an open door, just two doors from his own. He stepped inside and just missed being beaned by a mirror that a young man was removing from the wall. He stepped back swiftly, and the young fellow, with an apologetic mumble, took the mirror to another spot near the fireplace.

"What's going on?" He moved back into the room and found Nell at the center of the hubbub.

"Oh, hello, Charles. I wondered where you were today."

She smiled at him just as if she wasn't standing in

the middle of chaos, the bed in the middle of the room, the draperies down on the floor, and one young woman sitting on a chair mending a tear in the hem and two strong men grunting and red-faced as they moved a huge gilt wardrobe to another wall. A maid was at the hearth sweeping it while another young man grinned down at her and handed her a bucket of coal.

There was a general air of spring cleaning and a fresh start.

"What's going on?" he repeated.

"I'm moving . . . moving rooms. I hated my old drab room, and I thought I'd move to this one. I've always liked it, but it was reserved for guests in my husband's time. But there's no reason I shouldn't have it now, is there?"

"Good Lord," he cried, clutching his head. "No reason but that you should have already left Meadow House six months ago!"

Silence fell among the servants and Nell stood staring.

"Well, really," Charles said, exasperated. He threw his arms up in the air in a gesture of exasperation. This was the most ridiculous thing he had ever heard of. Perhaps she truly did mean to never leave Meadow House, as George had conjectured once. "You are . . . you're behaving as if you never intend to leave. George will not come until you do; you *know* that."

"I do know that, and the new Lord Simmons will have Meadow House in time. If you have forgotten, I have an ill child upstairs," she said, her expression stiff and resentful. "If you think I should move her and risk the fever returning then you are doomed to live on in delusion. We are going nowhere until I deem it right and safe."

"You had the opportunity to leave many times over the last six months, many times before Delphine fell ill again. I wonder why you did not?"

"That is none of your concern, Sir Charles." She glanced around at the servants, all gazing in interest at the two of them, quarreling. "Leave us," she said, then softened her imperious tone as she added, "just for a few minutes. I'll call you back when I need you."

Charles watched the men and the maids flee, a couple of them whispering to each other, and wondered what Nell had to say. He should have just left before saying anything to her in front of the servants, but he had been so taken aback by her behavior that he had blurted out everything he thought. Well, not everything, because he had just been wondering if her kindness to him had been motivated by a desire to get on his best side and perhaps convince him to help her delay his brother for some indefinite time from demanding his estate. She would not be so devious . . . would she? No, he wouldn't believe it.

"How dare you question me in front of my staff?" she said coldly, stalking toward him. "I will leave this house when I want. If I feel like taking the full year of my mourning, I will do it. If your brother likes, he can come and live here too. I'm not stopping him."

"You know that's not possible," he said, refusing to let her draw him into a quarrel. He gazed steadily into her eyes, softened his voice and said, "What are you doing, Nell?"

She stood stock still, gazing around her. "I . . . I hated my room."

Her tone had become uncertain.

"Yes?"

"And . . ." She shivered and rubbed her arms. "I wanted this room when I came to Meadow House, but Roald would not hear of it. It had always been a guest room so it would stay so, he said. I took the Red Room because he told me to, and that is where I lost . . ." She stopped, looked away, and bit her lip. "I bore Delphine there, and was ill there. I hated it, but Roald would never hear of a change. I'll be leaving this place soon, leaving it forever. I want some pleasant memories before I go."

Charles, his heart aching with the pain he heard in her words, stepped toward her and she melted into his arms, laying her head on his shoulder. "I understand," he said, rocking her back and forth, rubbing her back with one hand. "I understand."

"Do you?" she looked up at him. "Do you really?"

"Of course," he said, surprised to be telling the truth. "This has been your life for so long. You *should* have pleasant memories of it, and you should do exactly what you want."

"Just until I leave. I know it has to be soon, Charles, I know that."

Her face turned up to his was far too tempting and he touched her lips with his, gently at first, but she didn't move away. Nestled against him, she sighed against his mouth and he deepened the kiss, his whole body shuddering with new feeling and frightening emotion.

A tap at the door startled her; he could feel her quiver as he released her. She stepped back, her eyes searching, piercing him.

The door opened and her maid, Lundy, poked

her head in. "My lady, can we get going again? We're all milling about in the corridor. I have all your clothes to bring down the hall, you know."

"Of . . . of course," Nell said, wringing her hands together. She seemed to gather her wits and straightened her backbone. "Of course. Everyone can come back in. We have sorted things out. Haven't we, Sir Charles?"

Charles nodded dumbly, and as the serving staff flooded back into the bright room he fled.

FIFTEEN

In the dark every room looks the same, Nell thought, as she tried to fall asleep that night in her new beautiful, light, lovely bedchamber. What had she really been trying to accomplish by moving into a new room? To erase the memories of Roald and his lovemaking?

Maybe in part. It had never been her favorite duty in marriage, but he had been kind and thoughtful at first, and though it had not been pleasant, it had given her pleasure to give him such great satisfaction as he seemed to derive from the joining of their bodies.

She had been with child when Roald inherited the estate, and she lost her son within the first few weeks of moving into Meadow House, lost it in that very bed in the Red Room. But she had been young enough and hopeful enough that she had wanted to get with child again soon; she had always known that was why Roald married her. An heir was vital, and she was young and healthy. It had seemed so important, and she had wanted to please Roald so badly.

Everyone told her that was her duty, to please him and give him children. It would be her pleasure too, for she loved the idea of many children running free through the house, sliding down the balustrade, playing in the garden. Her sister had five children, and wrote letters detailing their antics. For some women childbirth seemed little more taxing than a few days of upset and a day or two in bed, and then life resumed as normal for them.

But it had been overwhelming and exhausting for Nell, a trial ending the first time in death and sorrow, and the second time in a premature birth with a sickly child. After Delphine, when Nell had pleaded for more time before reassuming her wifely duties, Roald had accused her of trying to avoid having his heir. And those same attentions had become little more than a punishment. She had hated it, holding herself rigid against his grunting pleasures. She had felt little better than a breeding sow, like the ones out in the piggery, exposed to the boar for one reason, and one reason only.

It had changed everything for her, but she had never been able to express any of that to Roald. He would have despised her, she knew it, if he didn't already. Ultimately she had had no more insight into how he thought or what he felt than she did a stranger on the street.

When it became obvious after a while that she would bear no more children, he had finally left her alone. With the distance of years she could see that he was becoming ill himself even then, but at the time, though she had been relieved when weeks turned into months and he no longer came to her room, it had felt like abandonment, too. And failure.

Changing rooms didn't erase all of that old pain and humiliation. Though Roald had been dead for months, she could still feel his spirit haunting the house, his disapproving grimace everywhere, with every change she made. So why was she holding on to the past, to Meadow House?

For one moment that afternoon, when Charles had looked into her eyes and said, "*What are you doing, Nell?*" it had seemed almost like he was searching her heart and seeking out her pain.

And when he took her in his arms, for a brief moment it had felt safe and loving and yet strangely disturbing. She had imagined other more intimate caresses, and when she closed her eyes and he kissed her, she had imagined lying back on the big ivory-draped bed and surrendering to desire. That she could picture all that frightened her more than anything.

She turned over on the bed and stared into the darkness.

Why hadn't she just stayed on the cot in Delphine's room? At least there she wasn't plagued by such fervent perturbations of the spirit. She turned over again and pulled the covers up over her. It was cold. And she could imagine another body there, warm and masculine, holding her close against his enticing nakedness.

Stop! She shifted again and hammered her pillow, then curled up in a ball to try to get warm. She was a widow and a mother, the mother of a fragile, frail child who needed her complete devotion. It wasn't right that she should be thinking of anything or anyone else, and certainly not of a selfish wastrel of a knight who disquieted her calmness and gave her midnight visions of forbidden diversions.

She would think of other things. She had been to Dorsey House a couple of times; she would amuse

herself with thinking of new curtains or wall-
coverings. Or new furnishings. Perhaps she would
redo all the ground floor rooms and then begin on
the bedrooms.

A new bed for the master chamber. A big bed.
Covered in velvet.

Velvet? Just for herself? But yes, pale blue velvet
and the finest linen sheets, soft as skin.

Sleep eluded her for most of the rest of the night.

Morning finally came, though, and she crept
from her bed feeling drawn and haggard. It was her
first night away from Delphine in weeks, and she
slipped down the hall and upstairs with just her
nightrail and dressing gown on, urged by her worry
for her daughter.

The door was ajar and she pushed it open, ex-
pecting to see Martha there. And she was, sewing a
hem in a linen sheet by the early morning light.

But there, sitting on the edge of the bed making
Delphine laugh, was Charles, the last person she expected to see up and about so early in the morning.

He twisted and gazed at her, taking in her disha-
bille with a grin. "Look at your mother, the sluggard!"

Delphine giggled, and Charles drew her up to sit
so she could see her mother.

Nell felt almost an intruder, but she padded
across the floor and leaned over to give her daughter a good-morning kiss. In doing so she had to
brush past Charles, and she could smell his shaving
soap and the warmth of him radiated over her like
a warm spring shower. Her breast brushed his
shoulder and she could have sworn his whole body
jolted, just as she tingled with awareness, her nipple

tightening. She jumped back from him as though scalded and he gave her a long, searching look.

Swallowing back her agitation, Nell said, "If you want to get your breakfast, Martha, you may go now. Sir Charles and I will stay with Delphine."

The maid curtsied and exited, and Nell sat down in the chair near the window.

"Mama, watch," Delphine said. "Charles, I want to show Mama the game."

"All right." He glanced at Nell and grinned again, a quirky smile she could find quite attractive if she let herself. He turned back to Delphine. "You begin, young lady."

Nell watched, entranced, as Charles engaged her daughter in a clapping game with a rhythmic chant. By the end of it Delphine was pink-cheeked and smiling, but out of breath. She wanted to immediately begin again, but Charles told her no, that she must sit quietly for a few minutes.

Nell stared at him. It was what she had just been about to answer, but he appeared to have an instinctive way of knowing that she was in need of a pause.

"Isn't that fun, Mama?" Delphine said.

"Yes, it is."

"I dredged it up out of my creaky memory," Charles said, with a self-deprecating grimace. "When I was just a lad I couldn't run with the other village boys to play, but sometimes the girls would play with me, and they taught me that game."

"He was lame as a child, mama," Delphine chimed in. "And the boys were cruel. Why are boys cruel?"

"It's just their way," Charles said. "Boys are

expected to be rugged and not to have any weak-
nesses."

"But the girls played with you," Delphine said.
"Girls are better than boys."

"Is that where you learned your way with ladies?"
Nell asked, with an arch tone, drawn in to the easy,
relaxed conversation.

He appeared bewildered and said, lightly, "What
flummery, my Lady Nell."

"Ah, but you have quite won my daughter's heart."

"Would that the older ladies were so easy to win,
Nell."

"The other one now, Charles," Delphine said,
having recovered her breathing.

"All right," he said, his attention returning to the
child. "But remember, you have to sit on the edge
of the bed for that."

He helped Delphine to the edge of the bed, and
her thin legs stuck out from under her white night
rail. He was so very gentle and yet encouraging,
and Nell felt tears form, though she quickly and
discreetly dashed them away. A rake and a wastrel?
She would never think of Charles that way again.

They played for a while longer, and Nell fell into
the game, too, but it soon became apparent that
Delphine was getting tired. Nell was just about to
say something when Charles once again foresaw
her concern.

"I think," he said, as Martha returned, "that you
ought to get a little more sleep, Miss Delphine!"

He stood, but she caught at his hand. "Charles,
will you visit me later?"

"Of course." He paused and gazed down at her,
then planted a swift kiss on the back of her hand.

"You sleep, little one!" he said with mock gruffness as he tousled her silky hair and straightened. He looked over at Nell. "Have you had breakfast yet?"

"No . . . I haven't."

"Then . . . will you meet me in the morning parlor?"

She hesitated, but then nodded. "Certainly, Charles." It would have been churlish to refuse, she told herself, as he left the room. She moved over to Delphine's bed, and the spot where Charles had been sitting was still warm. She would not dwell on that, nor on midnight visions and strange, turbulent dreams, nor on riotous physical sensations caused by the merest touch of his hand.

"You like your cousin, don't you," she said to Delphine, smoothing back her fair hair against the pillow.

Her daughter nodded sleepily. Martha drew the curtains and the room dimmed somewhat.

"He's nice. Can we see him when we go to London?"

"That is up to him."

"I asked him and he said it was up to you."

"We'll see, Delphine. A lot can happen. Do you mind leaving Meadow House? It has been your only home."

"But London is full of people, and things to see. There is a great park, and in spring people ride their carriages there and say hello to each other, and they wear the most fantastical clothes, Charles says. And there is a little lake where you can sail toy boats. Can we go to that park, Mama?"

It had been so many years since she had been in London for the Season. Was it the done thing to take one's child to Hyde Park? Well, even if it wasn't, she would do it anyway.

"We can certainly go to the park. Now go to sleep."

Delphine nodded and her eyes drifted closed. Nell stayed a few minutes longer, but then returned to her room to change into a gown suitable for breakfast with a knight.

She had the oddest feeling, as she entered the morning parlor, that she was a guest, and Charles the host. He had directed the table by the window to be pulled out, and it was set. At a signal from Charles the footman hurried away and returned in a few moments with a tray bearing the silver coffee urn.

"I heard you say you didn't like chocolate first thing in the morning. I feel the same, so I thought you might prefer coffee, as I do. In London I go to the coffee house for breakfast every day. My landlady has the most deplorable cooking skills."

They ate with just desultory talk of the weather—improving—and of the war—uncertain—and then at Charles's suggestion they moved to the library.

There, settled before the fire, a stool under her feet, Nell was in danger of becoming entirely too comfortable. Her sleepless night had left her feeling disoriented, but she battled that sense of bewilderment and fought to regain her balance in Charles's presence.

"How do you manage, Charles, to know just when Delphine needs to rest?" she asked, trying to focus on anything but her bewildering emotions toward him. "And how did you figure out that she needs moderate exercise to regain her strength? We have never discussed that, though I had come to the same conclusion."

He shrugged. "I was an invalid child," he said, staring into the fire. "After Nanny Lowell was pensioned off, for a time I was ignored, essentially, with just a nursemaid—the tyrant I spoke of to you once—who preferred to drink and drowse. Children are not thought to notice things like that, but they do. She eventually fell down the stairs, or something like that, and was discovered to be completely inebriated, and was let go. That was when Mary Llewelyn was hired. Welsh girl, very pretty, with a thick accent."

He smiled, and though his face was in profile, Nell could see his eyes mist. "She was different?"

"She cared," he said, simply. "She cared enough to ask why I wasn't out of bed. I was very young then, just six or seven, or maybe even younger, but she began to play games with me when her duties permitted."

"Games like the clapping game?"

"Oh, no, that was, as I said, learned from some village children, some girls; they were older than I and made me into a kind of pet, I think."

Nell smiled at that and thought he likely entranced them, with his thick curly hair and long lashes, his brown eyes and beautiful smile. She could imagine that as a little boy he would have been a very pretty lad, as he was a very handsome man. "You were speaking of Mary Llewelyn." She curled up in her chair and watched him as he spoke.

"She began to play games that made me move my legs. The doctor, I remember, was horrified and said I would be lame all my life—I believe he forbade me to try to walk at all—but she persisted. I can't imagine what courage it took, and what conviction, to keep going secretly, for I was told never to do so with my father or the doctor around. It was thought that I must keep my legs rigid and still for them to grow correctly."

"But Mary didn't listen."

"Mary didn't listen." He sighed and stared at the fire, the glow reflecting off his ruddy cheeks and handsome countenance. "Soon, I was out of bed and learning to walk properly."

"How wonderful! Was Mary rewarded?"

Charles's expression darkened. "No. No, she wasn't rewarded. The doctor came up to see me one time and we did not hear him coming, so I was out of bed and walking. He startled me and I fell. Mary was let go." He sat back in his chair, his face shadowed by the winged back.

"Oh, no! But you walked. Couldn't they see that that was a good thing?"

"The doctor said by teaching me to walk too soon Mary had twisted my foot even worse and that I would never walk properly, that she had risked my future by doing so. I only learned this in later years, of course, from George, who heard Father and the doctor talking."

Nell reached across the small table between their chairs and laid her hand over his, but then quickly removed it. It felt too right, too natural. "What happened without Mary there?"

"I was confined to my bed for a while, but by then they couldn't keep me there. You cannot watch a child all hours of the day, and I took to roaming the house at night when no one knew. I saw and heard much I shouldn't have, let me tell you."

Nell let that pass. His family secrets didn't interest her as much as he did. There was still so much about him she didn't know, but from what she did know, it was becoming harder and harder to reconcile his mission at Meadow House. "Why did you come here, Charles? Are you just doing this as a favor to George?"

He didn't answer, and just stared into the fire for a few minutes. A coal popped and he pushed the ember back in with the toe of his shoe.

"Charles? Do you not have an answer? It's not such a difficult question."

"Difficulty is relative, Nell."

There was silence for a few minutes.

"I . . . I suppose you were just doing your brother a favor, is that right?"

Charles stared into the fire and picked at the arm of the chair. "I told you I wanted to enter the army, didn't I?"

"Yes, you did."

"Well, when that was denied me, I'm afraid I . . . drifted, for want of a better word. I have an allowance, but I've always lived beyond it. As my father's son I had opportunities, and I always ignored them. I thought of myself as useless, and lived as if I was." He grimaced. "I've been self-pitying and feeble. There, I've said the worst of myself. Never admitted that to anyone before. I have been parasitic and purposeless and expensive, living beyond my means. I have gambled and drunk deeply, and let myself drift along with equally useless friends, convincing myself it was my due as a gentleman."

"We all have our faults," she said, gently. "And what has that to do with you coming here?"

His gaze swiveled to search her eyes. "Not you. What fault have you ever had?"

She thought about all the things she could say, but many of them were private, faults of resentment and anger, self-pity and bitterness. They were faults she had only recently recognized in herself, the kind of faults that only hurt herself, she hoped, though she greatly feared that without Charles to challenge her she would have allowed them to hurt her daughter, too, in ways she could not even calculate. She would always be grateful to him for awakening her to the danger of overprotecting a frail child. "I let despair taint my attitude. If it wasn't for Delphine I would have become hopelessly mired in bitterness. But still, I let myself become harsh and judging. And I forgot that I can't be everything to Delphine. I . . . I'm afraid I resented it when she was sad at Roald's passing, because I *wasn't* sad. You were right about that, Charles; as bad as it sounds, I was angry that she mourned when Roald died."

"Don't blame yourself for that. You never let her know how you felt, and you had a right to whatever you were feeling. You had so much to bear, Nell. You've done so much for your daughter."

"But I've risked her health . . . I was so frightened of a relapse, that I didn't do what you and Martha have done, let her exercise and grow stronger." She shivered and reached out to him. He took her hand and cradled it in his large warm palm, then kissed it. She stared at their joined hands. "I'm so grateful to you, Charles," she said, meeting his steady gaze. "So very grateful."

His expression, his brown warm eyes, made her

mouth dry out, there was so much unspoken feeling there.

"I . . . I still will devote myself to her," she said, stuttering back into speech and pulling her hand away with an awkward jerk. "Of course I will, but now I know I have to think of her future, too, have to plan . . ."

"What about your future, Nell?" he asked. "What about *your* future?"

SIXTEEN

"I . . . I have to go consult with Mrs. Howard."

"No, answer first, Nell," he said, reaching out and taking her hand back in his. "As admirable as it is that you have made Delphine your life, and as much as she deserves your care, is there to be nothing for you? Nothing for the woman?"

"What do you mean?"

She tugged at her hand, but he wouldn't let go and she would not get in a tug of war with her own hand as the prize. And yet it was disturbing the way he stroked and caressed her palm with this thumb, and the earnestness in his expression.

"What happens to you when Delphine has grown up and married and left you?" he said.

"I can't think that far ahead! I can only take things one day at a time, one week in advance. She's just a child . . ."

"A very intelligent child who worries about her mama."

"How do you know that?"

"We talk, Nell. She asked me what other mothers do, and if they spend all their time with their children."

"What did you tell her?"

"I said only very special ones, with very special children. But the answer didn't satisfy her."

"One day at a time," Nell insisted.

"No, think, Nell. There are more hours in your day than Delphine will ever need. Why not ask for something for yourself? Why not *take* something for yourself?"

"It's all I can do, Charles. It's all I can do to just concentrate on Delphine and making her well, for now." It was a plea, an entreaty from her soul to let her be, to leave her jagged emotions to mend. She didn't know what to think, what to say. He was asking too much if he wanted her to answer for the rest of her life. She bowed her head. "Just one day at a time."

"I've spent my whole life thinking only about today and the next. It's what made me who I am, selfish and irresponsible. But if I had a reason to, I think I could plan very well. I think I could plan for two."

What did he mean? She worried at his veiled meaning, not noticing that he stood in front of her until he drew her up and enclosed her in his arms. And as good as it felt, as much as she longed to stay there, she pushed him away.

"No! I . . . I have things to do, Charles. You may know nothing about running a household, but it requires the mistress to consult with the housekeeper, and that is where I'm going now."

She turned and left the room, wanting to run but not willing to appear so foolishly weak. And yet her heart was hammering as if she had raced all the way up from the village.

Rather than have Mrs. Howard see her so agitated, she retreated to her room and closed the door behind her, leaning against it, waiting for her heart to calm.

What was wrong with her? How could such a man as Charles, charming and handsome but aimless and a wastrel by his own admission, have such admittance to her heart? Was it simply that no one else in her whole life had ever taken such care of her? If that was it, then her foolish emotions would settle soon. That was not real, and could not last. It was the merest bit of gratitude for his goodness and solicitousness for her comfort.

And if it was anything else, if it had anything to do with midnight longings and deliciously forbidden thoughts, that, too, would pass when she was in London with people to see and new things to do. It was only loneliness.

Lundy entered from the dressing room beyond the bed chamber.

"My lady?" she said. "Are you all right?"

Nell moved to the table by the window and sat on a chair, her knees giving out as she sank down. Her hands were shaking as she laid them flat on her knees. "No, I'm not all right. Lundy, I'm getting foolish. The simplest kindness, the most commonplace courtesy by Charles Blake and I quiver like an aspen leaf. His scent, his warmth, his touch . . . what's wrong with me?" She clasped her knees to stop them and her hands from shaking.

Lundy stared at her, folding the linen pillowcase she had in her hand. She laid it down on the bed and sat on a bench near Nell. "Do you care for the rascal?"

Nell nodded.

"Do you love him?"

"No, of course not. He's here to see me leave, that's all."

"That wasn't the question, my lady, begging your pardon. Do you love him? Or are you falling in love with him?"

"That's impossible. No woman would fall in love with such a man."

Lundy sighed. "Again, that was not the question. I asked . . ."

"All right, all right!" Nell put up both hands to keep Lundy from repeating her question. "I'm fool enough not to know, but even if I am, it will come to nothing. He's here for his brother's sake, and I . . . I have Delphine to think of. No husband is in my future."

"Why not?"

Nell stared at her maid. "Lundy!"

Again, the tiny maid sighed with an exaggerated exasperation. "Women have been known to have a husband and a child at the same time, and be able to juggle both, as odd as that may sound to you."

"What do you mean?" Nell said, narrowing her eyes.

Lundy shrugged and stood. "Nothing, my lady." She picked up the pillowcase and refolded it.

"No, be honest." Nell stared at the lined face of her maid. They had known each other for many years, long enough that Lundy took liberties other mistresses would not countenance. But truth was seldom to be had, and Nell was of the opinion that it was a valuable commodity. If one would not be honest with oneself, then it was to be hoped someone else would care enough to be frank. "I know what you said and how you mean it, but I know you too well; there's something more. You've come this far, finish what you would say."

"It is just that . . ." She folded the pillowcase over and over and finally twisted it in her strong hands. "Your late husband, God rest his soul, was not a husband such as a lady like you needs. And you got in the way of thinking it was your fault he wasn't caring of you, that if you didn't have Delphine to worry over he would have loved you better. But Lord Simmons . . . he was just cold by nature. He wouldn't have cared for you no how, not even if you had given him that heir he so badly wanted."

Honest words, Nell thought swallowing the lump in her throat, and she had asked for honesty, but harsh too. It was easier, somehow, to think that if she had just tried harder, or behaved differently, Roald would have come to love her again. But was Lundy right? Was her marriage doomed from the beginning?

In truth, it didn't matter anymore; Roald was gone, and there was only Delphine and herself.

"It is immaterial, Lundy," Nell said, finally, taking a deep breath and relaxing her grip on her knees. They weren't quivering anymore. "By his own admission Charles is a do-nothing scapegrace. The last thing I need is a husband like that and it is foolishness to speak of it; I have no indication he cares for me in such a way." Other than his kisses, she thought. And the melting glances he warmed her with, and the feel of his arms around her.

"Well, Mr. Godfrey, his valet—and he ought to know—he says he has never seen his gentleman this way." Lundy nodded once, sharply. "He says Sir Charles is, in his opinion, in love with you."

"That's enough, Lundy. I will not listen to servants' gossip!"

"Then you will never know anything." On that, Lundy exited, closing the heavy door behind her with an emphatic thud.

Charles morosely stumped toward his own room, thinking that he was going about everything wrong. His task had seemed so simple when he arrived. He had merely to find a way to dispatch Lady Simmons from Meadow House as quickly as possible and all his debt problems would be over. Fail to do so and he was insolvent for the foreseeable future and wasn't quite sure how he was going to live. He supposed he could descend on the homes of various cousins or uncles on his mother's side, but it seemed a bitter fate, given his family.

The hall was dim and he fumbled with the doorknob, but then saw Godfrey descending from the upper floor. "What were you doing up there?"

Godfrey started and gasped. "Sir, you startled me!"

"Never mind that, what were you doing upstairs?"

Godfrey advanced to the door and opened it for Charles and followed him into the room. "I was, if you must know, sir, visiting young Willie, who is tomorrow returning to his position in the kitchen. I was . . . told by Martha—his sister—that he had some questions for me."

His valet's self-conscious demeanor was diverting, and he needed a diversion just then from his ham-handedness with Nell. Charles strolled to a chair by the window and sat down as Godfrey busied himself with a stack of cravats, folding and refolding them.

"Yes," Godfrey continued, with a swift glance at his employer, "Miss Martha said that her brother expressed an interest in going to London and becoming a valet, and asked would I speak to him, tell him what my duties were."

"And your acquiescence has nothing to do with a certain pretty nursemaid, his sister, to wit."

Godfrey's back was to him, but Charles could see the rigid line of backbone stiffen.

"I would never be so presumptuous," he said, his tone flat.

Charles watched for a moment, but the topic of conversation was a sensitive one. How did one deal with feelings of love if there was no hope that tender emotion would ever be returned? It was a subject intimately interesting to him at that moment.

Idly he gazed out the window. A steady rain had worn down the drifts of snow and there were even larger bare patches of grass on hillocks. Delphine was better now, the fever gone.

The brief idyll of family life and wintry splendor was over.

"Why are women so unfathomable?"

"I beg your pardon, sir?"

"Oh . . . sorry, Godfrey, I was wondering out loud." Charles turned on his chair and sat back, elbow on the table by the window, watching his valet work. "So," he said, his curiosity overcoming him. "What did you tell young Willie about life as a valet?"

He shrugged, and kept working. "I said if your employer carouses at night, then your evenings will be late, for you must see him to bed when he gets home, no matter what his state or his ability to walk in a straight line, or walk at all. Willie chose to laugh."

"Hmm. And?"

"I told him that there were good men in the world and bad men. Good men are not necessarily solvent men, and bad men may pay a better wage, but that one is always better off with a good man, even if one's pay is late."

Charles stared at Godfrey for a moment, but the man still continued working. When he was done, and the pile of cravats was folded to his exacting requirements, he turned. Seeing Charles stare at him he said, "Sir?"

"Godfrey, I have been thinking of this for some time. I have come to the conclusion that women are not only incalculable, but are much the colder sex, even if common knowledge says they are the gentler, warmer, more loving." He thrust his fingers through his hair and sighed, leaning on his hand.

"I think, sir, that unless one marries a girl in her first season, women come with complications."

"Meaning?"

Godfrey sat down. Charles recognized that oddity of his relationship with Godfrey, but who knew him as well? And whose well-being was more tied up in his own? What happened to him happened to his valet. In an odd way, it was more like family than many familial relationships.

"Meaning that Lady Simmons has not had an easy life, though she may have felt she would, marrying a man like the late Lord Simmons."

Charles puzzled out such an oblique statement. "All I know is that every time I kiss her . . ." He stopped and glanced up at Godfrey, but his valet was imperturbable. "This is to go no further, you understand? No servant hall gossip about this."

Godfrey bridled. "Sir! I would not dream of speaking of such things to Lady Simmons's staff."

"Good. Every time I kiss her, and it has only been twice, or maybe three times, she looks so . . . lost and scared. And this last time, just now . . . she pulled away and left as quickly as she could find an excuse. Why? I'm not a monster, am I?"

"I should say if she allowed the kiss at all, sir, that would indicate she finds you more than passing attractive."

"Do you think so?"

"I would wager a quarter's pay on it, sir," Godfrey said, with a wry smile.

"Why?"

"I beg your pardon?"

"What makes you so certain? You have never witnessed her behavior to me. What makes you so sure that she is not repulsed by me?"

"Well, by what you say, sir.

"And?"

Godfrey sighed and looked up at the ceiling. "All right, this was told to me in confidence by Miss Lundy, Lady Simmons's maid."

"I know who Lundy is. She's the fierce little mud wren who only seems to look at me to criticize. Or so it seems, anyway, when we chance to be in Miss Delphine's room together."

"Well, she indicated to me that in her opinion Lady Simmons is frightened of love. As a mother, she is convinced that all she will do in her life is take care of Miss Delphine, and if she can raise her daughter to healthy adulthood, it will be her only accomplishment worthy of the name. Love or re-marriage has no place in her life."

It confirmed what Charles and Nell had talked of, and what he had gleaned of her thinking. But how did one combat such a feeling? If one wanted to, that is.

"Miss Lundy says that guilt is Lady Simmons's enemy," Godfrey added. "She feels guilty any time she takes care of herself."

"Hmm. Yes, the moment I think she is truly re-laxed and enjoying herself, she freezes up and runs off somewhere. I suppose her worries are too deep to ever allow her to let someone else take care of her, no matter how much they might want to, or . . . or how much they might love her."

Godfrey sighed. "That, sir, is something I have no knowledge of. Women, as you said, are incalculable. But . . . but it seems to me there are many people who feel undeserving of love. It's not something your class thinks important—love, I mean—but . . ."

"But what?"

Godfrey shrugged and stood, resuming his more formal stance. "I don't really know what I'm talking about, sir. Love is a mystery to most men, I guess."

"Yes. And I . . . I have other concerns than love. Survival being one of them."

SEVENTEEN

"If we can send down to the village, now," Nell said, consulting with Mrs. Howard in the housekeeper's tiny closet near the kitchen the next morning about the house's store of sugar and flour, "then have one of the grooms take you and get whatever we need." She glanced down at a neatly printed list and checked off a couple of items.

Braxton entered the housekeeper's room just then, his handsome face tight-lipped as he held out a salver with a note on it.

"What is this?" she asked, as she picked up the note and opened it.

"It just came by way of the Duck and Drake's livery man, my lady."

She read the note and threw it down on the table with an exclamation of disgust. "Have Sir Charles come downstairs and meet me in the library."

"Yes, my lady," Braxton said.

She snatched the note up and took it with her, preferring not to leave it for the staff to read, and strode to the library, pacing up and down the room once she got there.

Charles came in and offered a tentative smile.

"I got a very abrupt message that you wished to see me."

"Read this," she said and tossed the note to him.

He picked the note up off the floor, where it had landed, and read it over, taking it to the window for better light.

But he knew what it would say because he recognized the handwriting, and it had clearly not come by post. It could mean only one thing; George, impatient with waiting in London, had come to Gloucestershire and was demanding his estate be handed over to him.

And he was right; George wanted Lady Simmons and her daughter to leave by tomorrow afternoon at the latest, and give the keys and all papers over to the estate steward in the presence of the current Lord Simmons's lawyer, who had traveled to Gloucestershire for that purpose.

Nell was watching him. Her blue eyes were flinty again, the color cold as ice, and her lips were compressed in a tight line. He handed her the note back but she brushed his hand away and the note fluttered to the carpet once again.

"Well?" she asked, crossing her arms over her chest, the lavender material of her dress rucking with her tight grip.

He took in a deep breath. This was the confrontation he had been dreading, and yet it was almost a relief that the hour had come. His nerves had been shredded by uncertainty. It would all be over soon and his life, such as it was, could resume. "Nell, you had to know this was coming."

"You're going along with this?"

Her tone was a shriek and he involuntarily

glanced toward the door, where he had no doubt several staff members were listening. "I didn't say I was going along with this, I just said you had to know this was coming. You've been stalling George since August, when he could have rightfully expected you to have made arrangements to leave. He won't wait forever."

"You are taking his side."

The absurdity of his situation unfortunately occurred to Charles just then and he laughed. He wasn't trying to take sides, he was just trying to be scrupulously fair; Nell had admitted that there was a long period through the fall and early winter when Delphine was perfectly fine, and by implication could have traveled. It was not George's fault that Nell had decided to linger long past the time she could have been expected to leave Meadow House. Certainly her daughter's health now was a concern, but George didn't know that. Her illness had not occurred until the very night Charles arrived.

He opened his mouth to try to reasonably point that out, but her scowl had darkened, her pale, pretty face twisted in anger.

"I'm not taking his side," Charles said. "But this is what I came here for, after all. He sent me to see when you would agree to leave; it's not an unreasonable request. But you've never yet agreed to leave."

She was trembling with anger. "I'll leave the moment I think Delphine is fit to travel and not one moment sooner."

"I know that, but . . . ."

"There is no further need for discussion. What more is there to say? I will not be rushed on this, Charles."

"No one was rushing you, Nell. If you had only left in a timely fashion . . ."

"Enough of what was and wasn't done." She stalked toward Charles and poked him in the chest with one finger. "I will not be bullied, not by any man. I had enough of that in my marriage and I am blessedly free now, free to do whatever I think is best for my daughter. Why anyone would think I would want to voluntarily enter such an arrangement of serfdom again, I don't know."

"What are you talking about?" Charles asked, backing away from the prodding finger. "I don't understand what you're . . ."

Someone tapped at the library door.

"What is it?" Nell shouted.

Braxton entered with the salver outstretched and crossed the carpeted floor.

"What, again?" Nell exclaimed.

He nodded, but offered the salver to Charles. "It is for you this time, sir, again from the Duck and Drake, a second message. And an answer is required."

It would be from George, of course. Charles took the note and moved over to the window to read it. Charles had one last chance, George wrote, even though he had been gone an unconscionable length of time and had made no effort to contact his brother. He must aid in the eviction of Lady Simmons and her daughter. If he didn't, George wrote, Charles would be impoverished for the foreseeable future, left to deal with his gambling debts his own way, and could forget about sponging from his brother ever again. Success, however, would be rewarded with not only

his debts being cleared, but a gratuity to be discussed further after the fact.

"He wants to know when you will leave," Charles
said, simply, looking up from the note.

Before he could fold it up and pocket it, Nell
snatched the paper from his hand and read it, her
expression tightening.

It was the end of any warm feeling she would
ever have for him, Charles knew. The wording of
George's note was too succinct for any doubt as
to his motives in coming to Meadow House. He
had been going to tell her, had tried to screw up
the courage to explain, but now it was too late.
When she looked up and met his gaze, he read
only contempt.

"Leave and take a message to your brother," she
said, her voice trembling. "I will move when Delphine is better in my own opinion and not a moment
sooner. He can storm this house if he likes . . . he can
raise an *army*, but I will not leave Meadow House
until I deem it right."

He nodded and turned to go. Nell watched him
with sadness, but it was for what she had thought he
was and how that had been betrayed. He stopped at
the door and turned back, but seeing something in
her expression, he was mute and left. She heard his
awkward step on the staircase.

She read the note again, and then crumpled it and
tossed it into the fireplace, where the banked embers
caught it on fire and it flared, then burned out. Just
like her feeling for Charles, swift and hot then burning to nothing but ash.

He was there because he had been bribed, because
he had gambling debts and likely other debts, and

needed them settled. It was bad enough that he came at his brother's behest, but to know it was to profit from ejecting her from the estate . . . it was awful and disgusting and she was terribly hurt, the ache centering in her chest, leaden and heavy.

She had thought he had come to care for her, but now she questioned every word, every tender gesture, every caress. Every kiss. Until that moment she had not understood how deeply she cherished that sensation of being cared for and cared about.

She wrapped her arms around herself and stared out the window, scenes flitting through her mind like a magic lantern show: Charles finding her weeping in the chapel and tenderly raising her up and guiding her to warmth and care, then kissing her with such passionate tenderness; that moment in the garden when she knew he wanted to kiss her, and gazed at her with such yearning; seeing him play with Delphine, a friend and almost a father figure for her little girl.

All motivated by money?

Impossible. But what else was she to think? If he had only explained, if he had told her how things stood with him . . . but now she was hopelessly confused, questioning everything, wondering if there had been a single genuine emotion or moment since he had arrived.

Charles trudged up the stairs, knowing that the moment had come as it always did when he would disappoint himself. There had been times in his inadequate personal history when he had determined to pull himself up and behave like a man should, and yet always that was the moment when his father had made sport of him, or after their father's death George had done the deed, and he would slink away and act the ignoble churl.

He limped into his room, sat on the edge of his bed, and called for Godfrey. When his valet emerged from the dressing room attached to the bedchamber, Charles said, "George has arrived in the village. I am deputized by her ladyship to go and tell him she will not leave until she wants to. What am I going to do?"

Godfrey strolled into the room slowly. "What you are told, I suppose. What choice do you have, sir?"

What choice did he have? He stared down at the carpet. There was always a choice, that was what he understood in that second. Even when he felt hopeless and trapped, there was always another choice for a man with principles and determination, but he generally made the wrong one, knowing in his heart it was the wrong one. He had an opportunity here to change his path.

Reflecting on the past weeks it came to him that the truth was staring him in the face all along. It wasn't that he *could* fall in love with Nell, it was that he already had. And there had been a moment when she loved him too, he was sure of it. But that was gone now, thanks in part to George's hideous note. And, if he was truthful with himself, due to his own behavior. If he had behaved as a man ought he would have told her the truth of why he was there and then disavowed his past behavior.

It was too late to win Nell, but it wasn't too late to be her champion.

Whether he thought her past behavior right or

wrong, in this instance she was completely justi-
fied. Delphine was still weak, and he trusted Nell's
judgment to know when it was right to move her.
Knowing that, he was given the opportunity now
to make a difference.

He looked up to find Godfrey's intent stare on
him. He frowned and said, "I will not let my brother
harass Nell . . . not now, not ever. If he tries, he will
have to go through me first."

"He will have his revenge, sir. Lord Simmons,
though not a violent man, will always find a way to
avenge wrongs that he fancies have been done to
him; you know that better than anyone. To so
openly defy your brother means certain penury."

Penury. What would he do?

"There is a man," Charles said, slowly, "a friend of
my father's, oddly enough, who is involved in trade
with Canada. He may . . ." He stopped and the full
idea formed in his brain. "For my father's sake he
may give me a position with his company."

"Work, sir?"

Charles sighed. Work. Getting up and going to
an office, and doing . . . something. All day, every
day. Drudgery, and uncertain financial gain. He
wasn't even sure what it would entail, nor how
much it would pay. He would still be in debt, and
with no place to live.

"You could find a wealthy wife, sir."

Charles looked up into Godfrey's eyes. "I don't
think that's for me."

His valet nodded, wisely. "Do you think there is
hope, sir?"

"No," Charles replied, not needing to ask what
Godfrey meant. "No, there is no hope that Lady

Simmons will ever look kindly on me again. She now knows I was bribed to come here and evict her and Delphine. What woman could ever look kindly on a man who would do such a thing?"

Godfrey turned and opened the wardrobe. "You will need your greatcoat, sir. It is wet and cold out there."

Reentering the world after so long at Meadow House was disorienting. He had quickly adapted to the ways of the great house—a state he would not have been able to fathom before entering it after such a long absence—and the village of Meadcombe seemed a bustling hub of civilization after the self-sufficient manor. He stabled his mount at the Duck and Drake and reluctantly entered, asking the landlord where his brother was and being shown a staircase.

He mounted, step after step seeming a tedious imperative bringing him closer to an uncertain destiny.

But finally there was no putting off the inevitable. He rapped on the door, and George's manservant, Victor, opened the door and ushered him in.

The room smelled of mint and camphor, and a pot of herbs simmered on the hearth. George was sitting well wrapped in a chair by the fire, with a screen between him and the actual heat. "Don't come too close," George said, as he met his brother's gaze. "I have heard there is fever at Meadow House."

Charles gazed at his brother, a pudgy echo of their vigorous father. No wonder the elder George Blake had been disappointed in his two sons; neither of them was the hale and hearty sportsman he was. "Scarlatina only, George, and that past the contagious phase. I never got it, you know."

"You could still carry the contagion. Sit over there." He pointed at a chair by the window.

Charles sat down and examined his brother. As always his complexion and robust frame indicated the truth, that George suffered only from rude good health. He was stout, but exercise would have mended his real weakness, which had resulted from the fact that George fancied every venue a source of contagion, and every new person a source of illness. He protected and coddled himself so much he often became a hermit in his London house. How he would handle country living and the strenuous business of dealing with estate business every day, Charles wasn't sure. But it wouldn't be his problem. He had his own new path to make, and he doubted he would see George again for years, perhaps.

With no preamble, Charles launched into his explanation to George. "As I said, there was fever at Meadow House, but it has disappeared without spreading further than little Delphine and the potboy, Willie, due to the wise precautions of Lady Simmons. That is not to say that Delphine is well enough to travel, though. Her health is precarious at best, and Lady Simmons will not move her yet."

"Another delaying tactic," George said, hitting the arm of his chair with his fist. "I cannot believe you have been so taken in by that woman."

Keeping his temper with difficulty, for he was in no frame of mind to be politic, Charles said, "George, I was there, I have seen the child daily. She is fragile, a tiny little thing. They are our kin! You cannot mean to eject our little cousin from her home when she is unable to even walk yet?"

"Who said she had to walk? Does Lady Simmons not have carriages and servants? One would think I was asking them to make her walk to London! I'm asking only my due, Charles; I thought you understood that when you left London."

Patience, Charles thought. There was a chance he could reason with his brother; it had happened on occasion. "I know you think Lady Simmons stalling; I thought so too. But in this instance she's right. The poor child is frail still, and her health . . ."

"Her health? What about mine?" He flapped his hand in the air and his manservant raced over with a vial of sal volatile and waved it under his nose. He recovered his composure. "I came down here at great personal cost, my dear brother, because I heard nothing from you and had no indication you were doing what you promised. I have suffered, I have traveled in hideous weather, I have feared for my life from highwaymen and icy roads, and I am not leaving. I expect you to go back up there and tell that woman to leave."

Charles stood and stared at George. He paced toward him and his brother shrank back in his chair, pulling his wrap up over his nose.

"Don't come near me, Charles," George said through the blanket. "Just go and tell the woman to leave."

"No."

"No?" George's shriek was muffled by the blanket but his eyes were wide with disbelief.

"No. I will no longer do your dirty work. If you wish Lady Simmons to leave, you must come up to the house, face her, and tell her yourself. And that would only be after you had engaged in a duel with

me and won. There is no other way to get past me
to Lady Simmons and little Delphine."

The sputtering behind as he walked out the
door told Charles that George was not prepared
for that answer.

EIGHTEEN

Shaking from the confrontation and his mind whirling as to what he would do once he got back to London, Charles needed the steadying influence of a drink and entered the tap room of the inn. It was a comfortable, ancient, low-ceilinged room, smoky and with the yeasty smell of beer.

"Ale, my good man," Charles said, approaching the bar and offering one of his last coins in payment.

The landlord himself, a vast man with a belly that hung down under his neat apron, served him with a foaming tankard and then sat down on the high stool from which vantage point he could peruse the entirety of the room. At that time of day there was only one other customer drowning his sorrows, and he sat on a low bench by the window, morosely watching the street scene.

"You be that gent upstairs' brother," the landlord finally ventured, his voice gruff.

"That 'gent' is the new Lord Simmons, and yes, he is my brother." He took a long draught of the ale.

"He be here to toss out poor Lady Simmons, then, right, and you his messenger?"

Charles sighed. It was inevitable that word would

have spread to the village even. "Yes, I am aught but his messenger. And a poor one at that."

The landlord eyed him. He leaned over and muttered, "I heard you was sweet on the lady, and she on you, that's what I heard. Lots o' kissin' and cuddlin' up at th'old house."

Charles leaped to his feet, his tankard spilling over and golden liquid splashing everywhere. "Do not spread such gossip, sir, unless you want to face me in a fair fight."

The landlord chuckled hugely, wheezing and coughing, enjoying Charles's outburst as some great joke. "Well, now, I'll take that as agreement." His gaze shifted to behind Charles. "What do *you* want, then?"

Charles turned and was met by a wall of man. He looked up to the face of the biggest man he had ever seen, surely seven feet tall and broad as well, his girth as large as the landlord's. The fellow had a red face and hands the size of stewing kettles.

"You Sir Charles Blake?" the behemoth said, his voice a growl.

"Yes, I am," Charles said, wiping ale off his hand onto his thigh.

"I am Nate Fletcher, and I'm here to beat you to a bloody pulp."

Charles backed up until the bar was at his back. "I b-beg your pardon?"

With the landlord looking on in amusement, Fletcher said, "I'm yer brother's attendant, don't yer know. He were a'feared of highwaymen on th'road from London, and I came along. But now I got a new job, seems loike."

The accent was purest London, and his look was

of the stews of Seven Dials. This was a man who had seen death often, and had perhaps caused some of it. "And that job is to beat me up?" If the situation had not been so absurd, Charles would have been afraid, but it just seemed too ludicrous to invoke fear. Surely George could not mean to have Charles beaten. A man the size of Nate Fletcher would kill him in a single blow, like a normal-sized man swatting a fly.

"If need be, though I'd not do it if ya acts loike a sensible bloke. You an' me, we're goin' up to Meadow House and I'm gonna escort her ladyship back to London, make sure she gets there safe. If you puts up any hindrance, then I'll be forced to do sumpin' rash."

Taking the measure of a man had been Charles's forte as a gambler. This man would be an efficient and inexorable fighter, and with his advantage of size and implacability, there was no way any man could win against him. If Nate Fletcher chose to fight, there would be no winning. Charles looked the giant over and said, "Before we resort to those . . . drastic measures, will you allow me to buy you a pint?"

Fletcher thought about it, his heavy brow beetled, then nodded. "Guess there's no harm in that, is there?"

"Two pints, landlord, on my brother's bill," Charles said to the innkeeper. "Mr. Fletcher, would you join me over in the corner, where we can talk?"

The two repaired to the corner by the fire, though Fletcher would never fit in the inglenook. Charles considered his words carefully, sizing up the man as reasonable despite his rough appearance. He had talked his way out of trouble before, having considerable experience with men hired by the owners of some of the more notorious hells in the backstreets of London. If approached right, some could be surprisingly sensible, though in this case bribery was beyond his means.

"What you got to say?" Fletcher asked, then belted back the pint in one gulp. His tankard slapped the wood table with a clatter. The man by the window looked up, then scrambled from his seat and left.

Charles signaled the landlord, who brought over another tankard to the giant and took away the empty.

"Are you married, my good man?" Charles asked.

"Nuh uh," Fletcher said, shaking his head.

"Oh." Disappointed, Charles said, "So you have no children."

"Didn't say that, did I? Got a couple."

Better. Much better. There was still hope that his first line of reasoning would work. "Have either of them ever been ill?"

Fletcher took another long draught of ale, but did not empty the tankard this time. He wiped his mouth with his arm. "Never sick a day in their lives."

Oh." Charles thought it through, covertly examining the man before him. "Let me tell you a story," he finally said. "A story of a gentle widow and her fragile daughter, a child so beautiful it hurts your eyes just to look at her. This child is frail, like a fairy child, her hands are so small and delicate. And pale! Her skin is so white it is translucent; you can see the veins pulsing through. Imagine this poor child, ill with fever, tossing and turning, calling out for the father who has left this earthly coil and whom she will never see again. And imagine the fear and pain of her mother, sitting by the bed day after day, hoping and praying that her little delicate darling will not die."

The giant was riveted, his big hands clasped before him on the table. "This little gal . . . is she the lady's daughter, th'one yer brother be so fussed about?"

Charles nodded mournfully.

"Will she live?"

"The fever has broken, but this poor fragile child has struggled her whole life against fever; some unknown illness plagues her and this most recent bout of scarlatina was such a close call . . . her mother still fears for her." Charles voice broke, but it was not all art. It had just occurred to him that with the current state of his relationship with Nell, he likely wouldn't see Delphine again, and that notion hurt. "Even as she recovers," he said, gazing out the window, "will she ever walk again? Run and play?" He glanced at Fletcher. "Will she be right in the mind?"

"The poor bairn!"

Charles nodded sadly. "And who is to say what moving her will do at such a time? She is already pining for her dead father, she has been sick most of her life, and now she's battling back from scarlatina. Moving her precipitately could be a death sentence, and what has she done to merit that?"

"Is that true? The little child could die?"

"I don't know," Charles said, truthfully. "But her mother is afraid for her, and Lady Simmons is a careful and caring mother. Delphine is all she has left in the world. It is simply cruel to expect her to leave Meadow House right now. If George could only see that! I know Ne . . . uh, Lady Simmons is ready to move to London the moment

Delphine is better . . . a matter of days, or a week. All she asks is time for her daughter to recover properly."

Fletcher rumbled under his breath, took another draught of ale, and said, "Doesn't seem too much to arsk."

"I don't think so."

"Right," Fletcher said, pounding the table with his fist.

He stuck out his hand to Charles and shook, squeezing enough so Charles knew that in this case discretion was most certainly the better part of valor. He would never have survived a fight with the mountainous man.

"I'll take care of it, sir," Nate Fletcher said. "I won't raise my finger to push the lady and her little girl out o' their home, you can bet on that. Fact, I think I'll just take myself back to London. Don't like doin' this kinda work if I'm to be used as a bully boy 'gainst a poor little bairn. Not a man's job, an' I don't mind if yer brother knows that."

Charles smiled in satisfaction as the man stood and demanded his horse be saddled. He waited while Fletcher made his arrangements, then climbed the stairs again to his brother's suite of rooms. Without knocking he entered to find George just where he left him.

"Before you deputize a champion, George, you should really check the man's constitution to be sure he is not as soft of heart as your Nate Fletcher, who, it turns out, is a loving father who will not see an ill child bullied into moving."

George turned in his chair and glared at his brother. "What do you mean?"

Charles strolled over to the window, watched while Fletcher rode out of the courtyard, and turned back to stare at his brother.

"What do you mean?" George repeated.

Charles sat in the chair opposite him. "Your bully-boy Nate Fletcher has ridden out on you, to return to London. When it became clear to him that you are here to evict a sickly child, his stomach turned and he left. Brother, you have no alternative; the household, and in fact the whole village, loves Lady Simmons. Unless you have access to an army, then you will be faced with several sturdy gardeners, stable boys, footmen, and various potboys and a few stout dairymaids, too, if you try to storm Meadow House."

George's face twisted in anger, his cheeks puffing in and out and turning red; his valet raced over, sticking the vial of sal volatile under his nose, but he swept it away. "Not now, you fool."

"Just wait, George. I promise you, when Lady Simmons decides Delphine is well enough to move—and the lady has already spoken of Dorsey House and her intention to retire there—then I will guide them myself to London. I sincerely believe the child to be recovering quickly. A matter of days . . . or a week or so at the most."

Silence.

Charles sighed, but then thought of a new approach, one that hit his brother where it hurt, and that was his own comfort. "George, if you go now and try to throw Lady Simmons out, you will have a staff that will leave en masse, and you will be faced with hiring a completely new household retinue." Charles was not sure of that—pragmatism would likely win out and no matter how angry they might be at George's behavior, the staff would likely stay at Meadow House, though they might be resentful of the new viscount—but he knew how to bluff, and he knew how important his personal comfort was to George.

It was a long few minutes. Finally George said, his tone resentful, "Fine. I am going back to London while this weather holds clear. But I expect you to make her leave the minute she is able."

"When Delphine is well enough," Charles repeated, his tone hard.

George glared at him. "Don't expect any reward for this, Charles, for you shan't get any. You have thwarted me at every turn, and you will bear the consequences."

Charles shrugged and headed for the door. "I expected nothing more."

Nell stared at the library fire and enjoyed its flickering warmth on her face and hands. It was almost dinnertime and outside it was getting dark. Charles had come home, she heard, and she awaited him, having left word with Braxton that she would be in the library if Sir Charles had anything to say to her.

Her disappointment in what she had learned, that he had a financial motive for coming to Meadow House, had abated somewhat. But it had still cooled the warmth she felt toward him, for she saw his actions now in a different light. Her heart whispered that she welcomed the cooling because her emotions toward him had frightened her, but she tried to ignore such treacherous murmurings.

The door opened and she turned in her chair to find Charles gazing at her as he crossed the room.

"Well?"

"George will wait until you deem Delphine well enough to travel. Then I'll escort you to London and see you settled properly in Dorsey House. In the meantime, George is going back to London."

There was some relief in that. She didn't think she had the strength to fight right then, and for Charles to intercede was welcome.

"Good. Thank you, Charles." She deliberately left her voice frosty. She wanted him to be in no doubt as to her feelings toward him.

He approached closer and she could feel the warmth of his body, a counterpoint to the warmth from the fire, and even more compelling. "No more than a cool 'thank you'?" he said, staring down at her.

"Do you think you have earned more?"

"I think I have earned your . . . regard, at least."

"Let us be frank." Nell gazed at him, keeping her hands calmly folded in her lap. "You came here to oust me for financial motives, because you have debts—gambling debts—that your brother promised to resolve. I won't ask what agreement you have come to with your brother, but I'm sure you will still benefit in some way. I will leave when Delphine is well enough to travel; that was always my intention, so what have you accomplished that I could not have by simply being resolute?"

"I've saved you the trouble of having my brother storm the house! It would not have been pleasant, I can tell you that."

"Ridiculous! That would never have happened."

"You don't know my brother! He may fancy himself

sickly, but where he thinks himself wronged, he is assiduous in getting his due."

"I think there are some traits that run in families," she said as she stood and moved away from him toward the door. "Again, I thank you. I think Delphine is well on the mend, and should be ready to leave in a couple of days."

She exited the library quickly, but as she moved up the stairs she had to remind herself to maintain a sedate pace, for she wanted to run. Despite all of her feelings that he was selfish and unreliable, she still felt a warmth toward Charles Blake that was entirely unsuitable. The sooner she could rid herself of his presence the better.

Taking dinner alone in her private sitting room she felt to be the wise thing, given the state of her nerves. She read for a while after, but could not have said the subject of the book at the end any more than in the middle. Moving from the Red Room to the Ivory Room had not made a whit of difference in how lonely and empty the house felt, and for a long time she just sat and stared at the glow of the embers in her grate. London had now become something to be looked forward to, for then she would be rid of the presence of Charles Blake and have things to distract her from her new awareness of how isolated and lonely she had become within herself.

At last, she decided to go up and be with Delphine for a while. She had let Martha resume her duties, and found that in some ways Martha was better at getting Delphine to exercise a little than she. It was still a battle that she fought with herself, for she would be too lax with Delphine, too fearful of a relapse, too protective.

But when she went up to her daughter's room it was to find Martha sitting in the corner sewing one of Delphine's nightgowns; sitting on her child's bed with a book was Charles. It was too late to back away, for she knew he had seen her. But he kept reading anyway.

Nell murmured to Martha that she could go have her evening tea with her brother in the kitchen if she liked, and she took the maid's chair.

The story he was reading was Delphine's favorite, The Gilded Knight, and Charles's childish painting was still propped up at the end of the bed. Though her daughter had waved to her, she seemed content to have Charles read her the story. There was certainly a novelty in it, for Charles supplied the voices in different tones, and even snorted for the dragon.

Roald would never have done that, Nell reflected, as she picked up the nightgown and began sewing where Martha had left off. Nor would he have sided with her against someone of power, and it had to be admitted that Charles had done that. Lundy had come in to her that evening with some wild tale of Charles facing a giant in her defense, but it sounded frankly like something from one of the fairy stories Delphine favored.

She laid the sewing on her lap and watched for a moment the intimacy of the scene, Charles's handsome face animated in the spill of lamplight, and Delphine's wide-eyed enjoyment of his performance. It was heart-wrenching and touching all at the same time given the recent tumult of her feelings for Charles.

When they moved to London Delphine would want to continue their friendship, and given his status as a relative, how could she reasonably deny him? And yet for her own peace of mind she would. Even if she had ever considered marrying again, he would not have been a likely candidate, an impoverished and wastrel knight.

And yet he touched her heart. And unless she was a very poor judge, he did care for Delphine deeply, and perhaps even for her, as well. Maybe someday, if he proved himself worthy, she could learn to trust him. But she couldn't foresee any circumstances that would bring about such an event.

From the moment Nell had entered the room, Charles had been preternaturally aware of her, every movement, her scent, her figure in the shadows as she sat and sewed. But it was the sense of loss that cut into him, the loss of her esteem and her determined coldness toward him now. What he had expected or hoped for, he didn't know, but it was clear all hope was over. She wouldn't even want to see him once they got to London, he was certain of that, and he would be too busy finding a position to do all the wonderful things he had talked to Delphine about.

Nell wouldn't need him there anyway. She was rich, beautiful, had an adorable child and her own house. She would be sought after not only for all of those things, but for herself, her spirit and grace, her lively mind and tender heart. She would meet old friends, worthy men would seek her out, she would find new life and maybe love.

Though no one would ever care for her as he did, valuing her feisty temper and strong will. Most men didn't value those attributes in a woman as he had come to. But ultimately, she would still be valued for her goodness, her perfection.

With a heavy heart he closed the book finally and Delphine clapped her hands. "That was wonderful, Cousin Charles," she said.

"It is time for sleep, young lady," he said.

She allowed herself to be tucked in. "Now tell me again about being knighted," she said, sleepily.

He hesitated and glanced at Nell, but she appeared to be concentrating on her hem.

"I think I'll tell you another short story instead," he said. He pulled her covers up to her chin. "But you have to close your eyes."

She obeyed and he turned the wick of the lamp down. Nell laid aside her sewing.

"Once upon a time there was a young man who didn't think very much of himself," he began, his voice quiet. "He was poor and lame, and thought others didn't like him. He often felt sorry for himself, which is not a good thing to do. So when a great prince noticed him and told him to come with him, the young man was greatly flattered." He knew Nell was listening, and he knew he was destroying, perhaps, what little respect she had for him, but it was time for the whole truth.

"But even if he was poor and lame, people could still like him," Delphine said.

Charles tweaked her nose. "If only the young man had been as wise as you! Unfortunately, he measured himself by the influential friends he could count. The prince made him a kind of pet, lavishing gifts on him and taking him to parties. But they were not good kinds of parties, and people often drank too much wine and became very silly as a result."

"Does drinking too much wine make you silly?"

"Excessively. What the young man soon came to realize was that many people didn't like the prince, and many of his worthwhile friends stayed away from the young man because he was now the prince's pet. He thought they were being idiotic because after all, who would not want to be with a prince?"

"Why was the prince so silly?"

Charles chuckled. "That is a question many people wiser than I have asked to no avail. But my story is about the young man, not the prince, who must find his own story. The young man was one night on his way with the prince and some others from one party to another, and they decided to walk. That was a grave mistake, for the prince, as I have said, was not at all well liked, and he was very noticeable, since he often wore a uniform, even though he was not truly an army officer. And he was a very big man, and very recognizable.

"To be brief, young lady, as I see even now your eyelids drooping, a disgruntled subject intended to pelt the prince with a particularly rotten piece of fruit, a very fragrant and melting orange. The young man, under the influence of too much wine, stumbled just then and the rotten fruit caught him on the ear. The prince was greatly touched by what he perceived as the young man's valiant behavior, throwing himself in front of a projectile, and told his mother, who then made sure that the young man was knighted in circumstances to make anyone blush, so eloquent was the praise and so majestic the ceremony."

Charles looked up to see Nell's gaze fixed on him. He shrugged. If it was not so painful to him now, he would have laughed. The one honor in his life that had been given him on merit, and it was all a silly mistake. Every time someone used his full title, he was reminded of that foolish time, and how soon after the prince had become bored with his company and sent him on his way with a particularly cutting remark.

"But . . ." Delphine struggled to stay awake and opened her eyes wide, staring up at Charles in the dimness. "But it was not the young man's fault such a mistake was made, and he should never feel bad for such a thing. Should he?"

"No, he shouldn't," Nell whispered. "Now go to sleep, Delphine, so that Charles may retire."

"Good night," Charles said, standing and stretching. He hesitated, but leaned down and kissed Delphine lightly on her forehead. "Go to sleep, and I will visit you tomorrow, when I expect that we will play the hand-clapping game again."

NINETEEN

Two more days saw Delphine's recovery to the point that Nell considered it safe to travel. If she was motivated to see things that way by her discomfiture in Charles Blake's presence, she would never admit that to anyone.

Delphine was plainly well enough to make the trip. Though still too weak to walk on her own, she was light enough for Nell or Martha to carry her, and in gentle stages, and with the weather continuing to cooperate, it was agreed that they could make it to London in two days, or three at the outside. If they were going to go at all, they must while the improvement in the weather held.

Charles had been amazed by the fact that Nell had already prepared some time before for the removal, and it was relatively easy, with the staff of Meadow House promising to send trunks on after. Nell and Delphine were traveling with Lundy and Martha, and Willie—or William, as the boy now preferred to be called with a new pride in his advancing position in her ladyship's household—and Godfrey were following with the luggage in a couple of days in the ancient carriage Charles had used to travel.

When the momentous day came there were many

tears. Mrs. Howard, the housekeeper, promised that if the new Lord Simmons was anything like his reputation, she would soon follow to London to take charge of Lady Simmons's household. Braxton, the footman, was stoic but had tears in his eyes. Charles suspected he had a too-personal interest in his mistress, but the fellow had never by deed or word been familiar that Charles knew of. And what man could know Nell and not fall in love with her? He was guilty himself.

Charles supposed he was happy the removal was finally taking place. He had been in a kind of Limbo while at Meadow House, neither resigned to hell nor admitted to heaven, though it had served a purpose. Seeing himself through other eyes had been bracing and had changed his view of the world and his place in it. Now it was his duty to go forth and change his life. Whether he could do it or not he wasn't sure. Having never tested his resolve, it was an unknown quality.

But that resolve was inflexible this time; he could not imagine going back to his old life. Dreary as it would likely seem to all his friends, he was changed. His metamorphosis was incomplete but advancing.

The day of departure was bright and sunny, but cold. That was a good thing, for if the temperature had stayed too high the roads would be soggy and impassable. This way even if rutted, the roads would be hard and navigable. The exposed grass in the fields was frozen into stiff tufts, and mud had solidified into brown ridges along the highway.

Because of the number of ladies inside the carriage, Charles was riding outside with the driver, and welcomed it. Being near Nell had become

unbearable. Remembering kissing her, knowing
he never would again, being aware every moment
of how low her opinion of him must have sunk,
and how irrevocably he had contributed with his
story of his knighthood: it was all too much to
bear.

The day wore on with just a few stops for re-
freshment along the way when hot tea became a
necessity. Desultory conversation with the driver
was all he had, but James was a taciturn type, and
so quiet most of the time. The noise of the carriage obviated much in the way of chatter anyway.
Charles had too much time to think, so he turned
his thoughts to what awaited him in London.

He would have no rooms, certainly, for he had
been gone far too long, and all of his belongings
that remained in the room would have been sold
for his back rent. Since his intention had only
been to be away one week and return, having
earned a reward, he had left many of his personal
belongings, including a jeweled stickpin of some
value, and a few other folderols. His landlady
would have more than enough, if she sold it all,
to pay for his rent.

So he would have to plant himself with one
cousin or another for a time until he found a position with his father's friend or whoever would hire
him. Clearly Godfrey would have to find another
position, and that pained Charles the most about
his new penury, because the valet was almost a
friend, they had been so close.

Which brought him again to Godfrey's suggestion of a marriage for money. It would solve all of
his problems, and his title and connection to other

titles was enough in some eyes to make him a worthy object. Many a young lady with ten thousand for a dowry would marry him with little in the way of wooing. It was not considered an unpalatable way for a man of meager means to make his fortune.

So why could he not go along with it? Was it because he still had hopes of Nell?

No, that wasn't it. She disdained him, and with all good cause.

Other better men than he had married rich ladies to improve their financial situation. Why not him?

He just couldn't see it. It didn't seem fair to saddle a young lady with his worthless carcass when he couldn't even promise himself to do the honorable thing, and try to fall in love with her. That kind of marriage, with little love and less respect, seemed far more dreary than working for a living.

He gloomily gazed off at the darkening sky, gray clouds rolling in and reflecting his gloomy mood. The road was indeed rutted and the temperature had risen as the day advanced, so it was becoming soggy, and the driver was concentrating all his effort on maintaining a good speed while keeping the bumping down to a minimum.

A rapping on the side of the carriage awoke him from his stupor, and he urged the driver to stop. He leaped down from the seat, landing in a puddle, and opened the door, poking his head inside.

"Everything all right, ladies?"

"Charles, Delphine is not well," Nell said, panic in her eyes. "How long is it to our rest stop tonight?"

He gazed at Delphine; she was curled up in a bundle of blankets. Laying on her mother's lap, her pale face was marked by two red dots high on her cheeks and a film of perspiration over her forehead. "Quite a while yet, a number of hours. Do you think this is a recurrence of her illness, or is it the motion of the carriage?"

Nell gazed down at her daughter, uncertainty in her eyes. "I don't know."

"Then let's stop at the next village and rest there. We'll not take chances with her health."

"Thank you, Charles," Nell said. "It's getting so dark. What time is it?"

Charles pulled out his pocket watch. It was only one in the afternoon, and should have been fully light. He gazed at the sky and noted the dark clouds he had only peripherally noticed before.

"Storm comin' in," the driver shouted down from his perch.

A wind whipped down the road and tugged and flipped the skirts of Charles's greatcoat. "We had better move along," he said, reaching in and giving Nell's hand what he hoped was a reassuring pat.

Martha's pale face was pulled in a fearful expression, but Lundy, as always, was impassive. She nodded to him. "We'll do, sir, if you can just get us to the next town."

"All right." He closed the door, jumped back up next to the driver and explained the plan, which the driver approved.

They were in the middle of an open plain, and when the icy rain hit, Charles felt the full force of it on his cheek. He pulled his collar up as they bumped along, and wondered how far they were to the nearest town or even village. It was an unfamiliar route for him, so he wasn't sure of his way.

The temperature was plummeting even as the icy rain slashed at them. The carriage jumped and jolted and the horses began to get restive; Charles was getting stiff from holding himself rigid against the wild movement of the carriage. He shielded his face from the rain and tried to catch a glimpse of the carriage driver to make sure he was all right. The man was hunched down in his greatcoat so far, and with his hat pulled down over his face, that it was a wonder he could see the road at all.

And perhaps he couldn't. The carriage meandered off to one side, one wheel caught a soft slump of muck, and in a moment things went from miserable to dangerous; the carriage jounced once too often, the horses bolted, and the carriage tipped, careening wildly down a slope.

Holding on to the side of the seat, trying to maintain his balance, Charles knew it was a losing battle. He heard screams, the landscape flashed by, the carriage tipped more, and he was thrown free as the vehicle finally came to a rest on its side. Charles lay in the ditch, the cold rain pattering on his back. He moved, tentatively trying to get onto his hands and knees. A sharp jabbing in his ribs made him cry out, but even more of concern to him was the stillness of the driver, who lay in the ditch, and the ominous silence from the carriage, the only sound a moaning and soft weeping.

He moved gingerly, sucking in his breath at the pain of every movement, and crawled in the muck to check on the driver. The poor man was in a ball at the bottom of the ditch, his face coated in filth. Charles wiped some away, enough to establish that the man was breathing but unconscious.

Struggling to his feet Charles saw, through the pelting rain, that the horses stood, their traces tangled but seemingly intact. They stood still, their heads down, almost human with an expression that looked like shame on their mild faces.

Shivering, wet, and filthy, Charles slogged through the long wet grass and ice to the door of the carriage, pulled himself up, and yanked the door of the tilted carriage open. It was getting even darker but he peered in, trying to see. One of the women wept quietly, with great moaning sobs.

"Is everyone all right?" he gasped. "Nell? How is Delphine?" He wrenched his head to one side and spat out muck that clogged his mouth.

"My lady is knocked out," Lundy cried, her voice quivering but strong. "Martha is all right but frightened—it is she who weeps—but Miss Delphine . . . oh, sir, she is pale as death!"

Charles struggled to maintain his calm. "But still breathing? Lundy, is she still breathing?"

"Yes," a new voice gasped, that of Nell. She took in a long ragged breath, as though the wind had been knocked from her. "Delphine is breathing but feverish, and I am recovering. Charles, what has happened? What is going on?"

"We have upset," he said, holding back a gasp at the pain in his side. He gazed down into the ditch in the growing gloom. The rain was getting worse, and a wind was sweeping across the wet fields, bending winter grass down flat. "The driver is unconscious, and I must drag him to some shelter; can't just leave him in this pelting rain and . . . oh, God, snow. It is beginning to snow."

"Oh, no!" Nell cried. "Charles, what are we to do?

Delphine is on my lap, but she's not awake . . . not . . ." She broke off, clearly trying to quell the panic in her own voice.

The weight of his responsibility descended on Charles. Care for these women was his duty, and a heavier one he had never known. It was his decision to make now. Go for help? Stay with the ladies and hope for a vehicle to go by? Try to bring the team together and pull the carriage upright?

A light in the distance brought to mind a farmhouse they had passed.

"What are we going to do?"

The trembling cry from the woman he loved with all his heart cut into him. "Nell, it's going to be all right, I promise. I must try to get the driver up near the carriage, to a bit of shelter. If you and Miss Lundy can take care of Martha and Delphine, I'm going for help; I see a light and a farmhouse near, I think. Then we will right this carriage and find some shelter." He sounded far more confident than he felt, and that was good.

"All right. Please hurry, Charles."

"We'll be all right, sir," Lundy called out.

Charles, ignoring the stabbing pain in his side, tugged and pulled the driver to a bit of shelter, and pulled his hat back down over his eyes. Poor fellow was still unconscious, but there was nothing more Charles could do for him that moment.

The next hours were a nightmare, but not without reward. The field was muddy but stiffening as the temperature plunged back down, and Charles slogged across it toward the beckoning light. There he found a farmer and his sturdy son just sitting down to an early dinner of potatoes and bacon, but they left it to get cold on the table when they heard of Charles's predicament and that of the ladies.

Charles vowed to himself to send them recompense for their great kindness and stoic, silent help. They helped the ladies from the carriage, their oxen team righted the vehicle, and they assured him that the axles were fine and the body intact. Once Charles indicated his determination to move on to the village, which was close by, the farmer assured him, not much beyond his own house, they checked the team and pronounced the horses no worse for the accident, and hitched it up "all right and tight," as the red-faced farmer put it.

They offered the shelter of their tidy farmhouse, but Charles was too worried; he needed more than a farmhouse and wanted the security of a village and at least an apothecary to tend to the ladies and to the carriage driver.

Charles, with the aid of that sturdy farmer's son, gently placed the coach driver in the carriage with the ladies, and drove the team himself to the inn, which was on the near side of the village. He pulled under the portico, and while grooms rushed out to care for the horses, he opened the carriage and helped out the driver, who had since regained consciousness and shamefacedly limped into the inn.

Nell was going to carry Delphine but Charles put one hand on her arm, staying her action as Lundy clambered from the carriage.

"Let me," he said. "Let me carry her in."

Nell's returning gaze was searching, but she climbed down and let him pick her up.

As Charles hefted her in his arms—she felt

unaccountably heavy to him, when he knew she was light as a feather—she opened her eyes.

The sun was near the horizon, but the storm was finally clearing and one ray of brilliant sunlight peeked through the clouds and slanted to them across the countryside.

Delphine reached up and touched his hatless head. "My gilded knight . . ." she murmured. "You really are my gilded knight, Charles!"

Nell, her eyes tearing, saw what her daughter meant, as the sun sparkled off his golden, ice-encrusted hair and greatcoat, the glitter like gold.

"Let's get you safe and warm, little one," he grunted, his expression twisted with emotion or pain, Nell couldn't tell which.

The next hour was a blur of bustle.

Once safely in bed Delphine recovered somewhat, but was thoroughly exhausted. Martha, ashamed of her earlier fear, vowed she would not leave Delphine's bedside that night, though a local physician said she would be fine after a rest. It was his opinion it was just the stress and fear of the storm and journey that had made Delphine vulnerable again. Now safe and warm, she seemed fine, just exhausted.

Lundy was fast asleep on a cot in the corner, Delphine was in bed, and Martha was in a chair, slumped by Delphine's bedside. Nell tiptoed out of the room, leaving all to slumber and rest. For herself, she was agitated and needed to know that Charles had taken no harm from the turmoil of the day.

She found his room from the landlady's instruction and tapped, then entered, intent on thanking him as he deserved for so valiant a rescue. But as she entered she found he was not alone, and his outcry of pain as the doctor attended him rent her heart.

"What is it?" she cried.

The physician looked up from his work, which was taping the young knight's ribs. "Ah, my lady, now *here* is where the true damage was done, for though the rest of you, even your coachman, will recover with no ill effects, Sir Charles here has cracked a rib, I think, or more than one, though I am no surgeon, you understand."

"Oh, Charles," Nell said, swiftly crossing the distance between them to where he sat, on the edge of his bed.

He grimaced. "It's nothing, Nell, please don't worry."

"How did it happen? And why did you say nothing? You must have been in pain."

He was silent. The doctor, however, an old man, gaunt and gray-thatched, was verbose. "Fool was thrown from the carriage when it tipped and cracked his head and his side. Lucky he is so hardheaded, for he would have fainted if his head was softer." He finished his job and patted Charles on the back. "That will do you until you get to London tomorrow, but see someone there, for this is only my diagnosis." He stood and put away his tools and tape in his bag.

He gave Nell a curious look, for she knelt still by Charles's side. "I'll leave him in your keeping, my lady." He straightened, one hand to his back. "Take good care of the young fellow."

"I will." She stared up at him, wondering at the strange amalgam that made up Sir Charles Blake, the mixture of selfish and selfless, kind and crusty, weak and strong. But in every case the good characteristics won when they were needed. His kindness shone when Delphine needed a friend, and now Nell had seen his strength, there for her daughter and even for herself to rely on when the moment called for great self-sacrifice and decisiveness.

The door behind them closed as the doctor exited.

Did she dare, Nell wondered? Was she strong enough now to let go of all her fears and be honest for the first time, honest enough to admit that she loved Charles Blake?

TWENTY

The expression in Nell's eyes overwhelmed Charles with terror, but the fear was that it could not possibly mean what it seemed. Her lovely face was filled with love shining from her blue eyes and radiating from her lithe form. It was all he had ever hoped for and what he knew he had longed to see for some time now.

But temporary likely; surely it was just gratitude, too easily confused with love.

"Is . . . is Delphine going to be all right?" he asked, wincing at the pain he now felt quite thoroughly.

Nell nodded, her eyes glittering with unshed tears. "It was just the carriage motion that made her sick, the doctor thinks. I believe he's right. It does make some people ill, you know. She's sleeping quite peacefully now."

"Are Martha and Lundy well?"

"Yes. Charles . . ." She seemed as if she wanted to go on but she stopped and just stared up at him.

He gazed down at her, knelt by his feet, and he wanted to believe in what he saw there, the adoration shining in fathomless blue, but it was too much to hope for. Too much. More than he deserved, and almost as much as he wished for.

"What you did, the sacrifice . . ."

He waved it off. "Nell, please, don't."

"Will you not let me thank you?"

"It's not that . . . but you would not have been on the road if not for me."

Nell sat back on her heels and stared in surprise. "It wasn't you, it was your brother who wanted us to leave. And Charles, if you come down to it, I should have moved to London in September. I considered it, knew it was right, but convinced myself otherwise. And then convinced myself it was for Delphine's sake when it was all along my own fear. And stubbornness. Your brother's letters were really abominable and set my back up to not give in to him, idiot that I was."

He shrugged and gasped at the knife of pain in his chest.

She reached up gentle hands and stroked the bandaged part of his chest. Her fingers lingered and touched his skin, stroking the fine blond hair on his chest above the bandage. "You should never have done all you did with cracked ribs. When I think . . . Charles, you dragged the driver, walked to the farmhouse, drove the team, and then carried Delphine . . . you could have hurt yourself worse."

Her voice was curiously clogged and thick, and he stared down at her. The gentle touch of her hands on his bare flesh was making him almost crazed, and the tension in his frame shook him. He shivered with longing. She reached up and framed his face in her hands. For a long minute they just gazed at each other. Awkward as it was, he never wanted the moment to end because it was filled with potential; in that minute he could believe that if he worked hard, he could someday earn her trust and love.

He saw the resolution on her face a split second before it was affected, but still didn't know what it meant until she lurched at him and pushed him down on the bed and covered his mouth with her own.

"Charles," she gasped between kisses. "I was wrong to ever doubt you." More kisses. "I felt . . . felt I could love you but then . . ." More kisses. "Then I . . ."

"Shush," Charles said, and took her in his arms. Pain wracked him but there was no way he was going to show how much he hurt, because then she would let go of him, and that pain would be so much worse. He held her close and stared into her eyes, overwhelmed by the trust he saw there. What had he ever done to earn that? A single instance of heroism in the carriage?

But it was no time for doubts. "Nell, I love you. I adore you. I want . . ."

"Kiss me more," she urged, closing her eyes and pursing her lips.

"Wait! I have to tell you . . ." He held her at bay, clutching her shoulders as they lay together on the lumpy inn bed, the light of a lamp on the table the only illumination. She opened her eyes and stared into his, her beautiful blond hair spilling across the covers, her pale pink dressing gown infusing her glowing skin with radiance. He wanted to clutch her to him and never let go, but he had to say something. He lurched up on one elbow and gazed down at her.

"It's like one of Delphine's fairy tales. You know . . . a selfish prince who thought the world owed

him a living until one lovely queen and her
adorable princess daughter taught him how empty
his life was, what a farce his life had become." He
shook his head and gave a groan of exasperation.
What bosh it sounded coming from him! A fine
speech, but it sounded like it came from the worst
kind of novel, the ones where people declaimed
their love with fine sentiments and shallow words.
Better to speak plainly. "Nell . . . I love you," he
whispered, his voice hoarse.

She smiled up at him. "Then kiss me."

"In a minute. Look, Nell, I know I'm not good
enough for you and Delphine . . ."

"Shut up, Charles, and kiss me."

Everything was rushing fast, like a river after tor-
rential rain, flooding and tumbling and torrents
pouring when a trickle had been there before. He
surrendered. "Nell," he gasped out, kneading her
tender shoulders through her gown, "I adore you
and I want to marry you; will you marry me? I will
work; I *want* to work. Odd. Not like me to be saying
that, but it's true, and I had a plan when I knew I
was coming back to London, and I . . ."

"Charles, work, don't work, it doesn't matter . . . just
shut up and kiss me." She threw her arms around him
and pulled him down to her.

The flood of tumbling words and emotions had
cleansed him and he knew love wasn't a matter of
earning or deserving, it just was. And foolish pride
or excessive humility would not gain either of them
what they wanted. He surrendered, touching her
mouth with his first tentatively, then hungrily, their
lips melding, their bodies fused on the lumpy bed.
A feather mattress could not have felt softer.

At least at first.

"Charles, you're groaning," Nell muttered against his mouth.

"What? I am?"

"Yes." She opened her eyes, stared at his face and then drew back. "Lord, Charles, your ribs. I forgot!" She sat up and helped him sit too. "Foolish man. Why didn't you push me away?" She tidied her wild hair.

He laughed then, groaning at the end of it.

"What is it?"

"As if I would ever push you away! How could I, when I have been longing to kiss you for . . . since the last time I kissed you. Since before you found out about . . . since before that hideous note from George."

She was silent and grave.

He grimaced at the pain in his chest, but soldiered on. There was so much to say, so much to explain . . . He sat on the edge of the bed, holding his side and talking through the pain. "I did come for money, you know. I have been a gambler, Nell— you may as well know the worst of me—and George promised to pay off my debts if I would come down to Gloucester and find a way to urge you out of Meadow House."

"Go on."

"But I soon found . . . you and Delphine . . ."

She was silent, watching him, grave but wide-eyed and waiting.

"I remembered you as a cold, hard woman, sickly, unhappy . . . and you probably remembered me as that drunken wastrel I was when I visited soon after Delphine's birth. But I soon saw the real you. You're so strong; but I saw how much you were sacrificing for your daughter, and I wished I could make you see that you shouldn't give away all of yourself. I wanted to give you so much, more than I have, anything I ever could. And I fell in love with you."

Her expression melted from gravity to tearful sweetness. She put one hand on his cheek. "I tried to resist. I couldn't be falling in love with you; I told myself that over and over. It was impossible. You were entirely unsuitable. And I didn't want love . . . certainly didn't want a husband. But your warmth . . . it was like facing the sun after being stranded in the Arctic. My heart was frozen but you thawed it and it beat and I felt it for the first time, felt what it was to fall in love."

He searched her eyes. "Do you . . . can you possibly . . ."

"Yes, Charles, of course. I love you."

A clock somewhere chimed midnight, and it broke the spell as if it were an enchantment in a fairy story.

"I . . . I have to go back and check on Delphine," she said, standing. "Martha is there, but the poor girl is likely sleeping by now, she is so wretchedly tired."

It had to be enough for the moment. He didn't have the nerve to ask again if she would marry him. She had never answered and loving him didn't mean she would marry him. After all, she had just said she didn't want another husband, but he couldn't see having her any other way than in matrimony. She was not the kind of woman one asked to be your mistress.

"May I come and say good night to her?"

Nell gazed at him steadily and then bit her lip.

"Charles, why don't we ask for her permission to get married? She's the only one you have to convince now."

As if the breath had been sucked from him, he gasped. "You mean . . ."

"Of course," she whispered, falling on her knees at his feet. "Scapegrace. I love you; what else matters? And if you keep kissing me as you have been tonight, I shall disgrace my position as a widow and mother. You had better marry me to keep me honorable."

"But is it too soon after . . . after her father's death for Delphine to accept?"

Again Nell reached up and cradled his cheek with her hand. "She loves you very much. I've never seen her as she is with you, and you're so good for her. Why don't we see what she says . . . how she behaves? We'll know soon enough."

His life, his future, was held in the delicate hands of a child.

Nell helped him into a shirt, pausing to kiss him soundly in the act, and they lingered for long minutes, touching and kissing, but then she broke away with a mischievous grin. "There we go again," she whispered. She rested her forehead against his, breathing raspily. "We had better leave this room, or you shan't be fit for company."

They made their way to Delphine's room. Martha had moved, curled up on another cot near Lundy's in the corner, and her snores indicated she would not be awoken easily. Nell put the candle on a table near the bed and knelt down at her daughter's side, and Charles grunted as he knelt beside her.

"We can't wake her up," he said, gazing at the

pale face. "Let her sleep. She's been through so much."

Delphine's eyes fluttered open just then and she reached out, spilling her doll onto the floor. "Charles? Did I dream? I thought we were in a carriage, and then there was a storm and the carriage tipped . . ."

He picked up her doll and tucked it back in her arms, then touched her cheek, marveling at the pale perfection of her skin. "All true, little one. We *were* in a storm, but we're at an inn now, halfway to London. You were so very brave."

"You carried me in, and you were all coated in ice. I remember now."

"You called me your gilded knight."

She nodded.

"Darling," Nell whispered, cuddling closer, the three of them huddled together in a knot in the dimness of the chilly inn room. "Do you love Charles?"

Delphine nodded again, and reached out and took his hand.

"So do I," Nell said, taking his other hand and completing the circle by taking Delphine's free hand in hers. "And we've been talking about it, and we were thinking . . . what would you say if . . ."

"If I came to live with you," Charles blurted out, when Nell paused. "If I married your mama and came to live at Dorsey House in London with you both."

Delphine was wide-eyed for a moment, and Charles feared he said too much, rushed such shocking news. Was she ill? Should he have held back?

"Could you?" she squealed. "Could you come live with us? And marry Mama?"

"Hush," Nell said, glancing over at Martha, who stirred uneasily but stayed asleep. Lundy's eyes opened, but then blinked back shut, tightly. "Yes, he could."

Delphine, her pale brow furrowed, thought about it, chewing her lip just as her mother sometimes did. "Would that mean . . ." She looked into Charles's eyes. "Would you be my papa, then?"

He took in a long, slow breath. "Would you want me to be your papa?"

She nodded, her eyes bright.

"Then I would be honored above all things." He leaned over and kissed her forehead.

She released his hand. "Now kiss Mama!"

He gazed at Nell and whispered, "Shall I kiss you, madam, or will it make us improper?"

"I'm going to be your wife, Charles, soon, I hope. There's nothing improper in that."

He leaned over, kissed her, and murmured against her lips. "We shall see about that."

"Now we're a family," Delphine announced with satisfaction. "Now we are a family."

ABOUT THE AUTHOR

Donna Simpson lives with her family in Canada. She is currently working on her next Zebra regency romance, LADY SAVAGE, which will be published in June 2005. Donna loves to hear from readers and you may write to her c/o Zebra Books. Please include a self-addressed stamped envelope if you wish a reply.